Scottish
Folk Tales
for Children

Scottish
Folk Tales
for Children

Judy Paterson

Illustrated by Sally Daly

The History Press

For Oscar and Maya,
my grandchildren.

First published 2017
Reprinted 2019

The History Press
97 St George's Place
Cheltenham, Gloucestershire, GL50 3QB
www.thehistorypress.co.uk

© Judy Paterson, 2017
Illustrations © Sally Daly, 2017

The right of Judy Paterson to be identified as the Author
of this work has been asserted in accordance with the
Copyright, Designs and Patents Act 1988.

British Library Cataloguing in Publication Data.
A catalogue record for this book is available from the British Library.

ISBN 978 0 7509 6844 7

Typesetting and origination by The History Press
Printed and bound by TJ International Ltd, Padstow, Cornwall

MIX
Paper from
responsible sources
FSC® C013056

Contents

About the Author

Judy Paterson is a professional storyteller and published writer, mostly of children's books. Previously a teacher, and headteacher, she is passionate about heritage, the need to preserve it and to make it accessible to children.

Judy has travelled far and wide as a storyteller but her first love is for the stories of Scotland.

Acknowledgements

I wish to thank all my fellow storytellers who, over the years, have inspired and encouraged me, and, in particular, Senga Munro and Dr Donald Smith. I was lucky enough to have known Duncan Williamson and Stanley Robertson.

Retelling a story in written form is so different from the spontaneous experience of sharing a story in the oral tradition when audience interaction influences the style of telling. I owe special thanks to Jeanette Sharp, who edited my first draft with the keen attention of a constructively critical audience of one!

Thanks also to my illustrator, Sally Daly. It was a great joy to work with her and opening her sketchpad was like opening a box of chocolates!

As always, thanks to my husband Mike and my long-suffering family and friends who allowed me to retreat from the real world while I lived in Fairyland.

Foreword

When living and working as a teacher in Papua New Guinea, Judy Paterson became acutely aware of the cultural, educational and social value of traditional stories. Perhaps it was more surprising on arriving in Scotland to find that her new home was also rich in traditional tales. Recovering and telling these stories became an important part of her personal and professional work over recent decades.

During this period there has been a cultural renaissance in Scotland, and Judy has been able to bring her combined talents as a children's writer and storyteller to the party with great success. In addition to storytelling in innumerable venues, and running workshops, Judy also found time to pioneer Storyboxes in Scottish schools. They were skilfully designed to enable staff to gain confidence in sharing stories as living experiences and to move seamlessly to participative activities. Judy has been very active in supporting emerging storytellers of all ages, but her passion is to encourage children and young people to become tellers and to keep the oral traditions alive.

Alongside all this, Judy is a skilful horsewoman. I have always felt that the magic she senses in these classic tales is akin to the organic life she attunes to in her beloved horses. The oral story is a living creature and helps us connect with our own energies and those of the natural world. That is where the sense of wonder comes in – amidst the drama, suspense and humour – and it unifies this whole collection.

Judy has chosen wisely from across Scotland, and has crafted versions of these tales that delight eye, ear and tongue. The stories are accessible for today yet also give a true flavour of their original contexts and purpose.

It has been a great personal pleasure to work with Judy over many years. I am delighted to see this, her new classic collection of Scottish tales for children. I commend it warmly to everyone who loves authentic stories and their telling.

Dr Donald Smith
Director, TRACS
(Traditional Arts and Culture Scotland)

Introduction

Before there were books, stories were told or sung in ballads; story songs. So as you read these stories, imagine I am *telling* you the story without a book, sitting by a fire maybe, on a long, dark night. I am not very good at singing!

These are just some of the stories I tell but they are some of my favourite Scottish folk tales.

The Witch of Fife

FIFE

Quhare haif ye been, ye ill womyne
These three lang nightis fra hame?
Quhat garris the sweit drap fra yer brow
Like clotis of the sault sea faem?

James Hogg – The Queen's Wake

Long, long ago, in the Kingdom of Fife, there lived a guidman and his very strange wife. The man was a quiet and respectable person, but his wife was carefree and flighty. Indeed, she was so odd that some of the neighbours thought she might even be a witch!

While they sat by their fires in the early evening the neighbours sometimes saw the woman disappear into the gloaming and often she stayed out all night. When she returned in the morning she was pale and tired but she never told anyone where she had been. She never even told her poor husband what she had been doing. Try as he might, he could not find out where she went. Each time he caught her slipping through the door she was gone by the time he followed her.

One night the worried man decided to wait up for her return. As soon as his wife came in through the door he jumped up.

'I have to know, Wife, whether or not you are a witch,' he asked.

'Indeed I am!' she replied, as she hung up her damp cloak.

The poor man felt his blood run cold. 'Dearie me, this is a very serious matter,' he said. 'If you are found out you will be caught and put on trial. This is terrible.'

'No it is not!' laughed his wife. 'I am not a wicked witch. If you promise not to speak of this I will tell you about my midnight adventures. You will see I do no harm.'

So the old man promised to keep the secret and asked where she had been that long night.

'I met four of my friends down by the kirk,' she told him, 'and we mounted branches of the green bay tree and stems of hemlock. These changed into magic horses and we rode, swift as the wind. We chased foxes and weasels and flew past the owls hooting in the dark. Then we flew over Loch Leven and rode to the Lomond Hills and what do you think we found there?'

The old man shook his head. He could not believe what his wife was saying.

'Well, Husband, we had beer to drink from little horn cups that were made by fairy-folk. There was a wee, wee man with a set of bagpipes and the music was like no other we've heard. It was so wonderful that the silvery trout in the loch below were jumping and the stoats crept out of their holes. Even the corbie crows, the grey curlew and the blackbird listened. And all the time we witches danced and danced and danced.'

'What good was this to you my weird, weird wife? Dearie me, you'd have been better off in your bed all night,' he replied.

When the next new moon rose in the night sky the unhappy husband watched his wife step out into the darkness. He picked up his cosy red nightcap and pulled it down over his ears. He sat by the fire and he was still there at dawn when the cockerel crowed. At that very moment his wife skipped in through the door. She sat by the hearth as she began her story, warming her cold fingers.

'We took cockle-shells for boats last night and sailed over the stormy seas; while the thunder growled and the sea fog howled, we flew as fast as the gale. Then we rode invisible horses fashioned from the wind carrying us over mountains steep and valleys deep. We soared across snow-covered lands where reindeer run and glaciers glittered in the moonlight.

And then we reached Lapland, a land all covered with snow.'

'That doesn't sound very exciting,' said the old man.

'Oh but it was!' cried the old lady jumping up. 'All the fairies and mermaids of the North were holding a festival with warlocks, other weird women and phantom huntsmen. And there we were, the witches of Fife, dancing and singing and feasting with them all.'

The old lady jigged around the room and laughed, 'Why, Husband, we learned the most amazing secrets while we were there. We learned magic words to carry us through the air. We learned more wonderful words that unlock bars and bolts. Imagine it! We can go wherever we want!'

The old man was too tired to imagine anything but his cosy pillow, 'Dearie, dearie me, what took you to such a land? You'd have been better off in your warm bed all night.'

The weeks passed and again a new moon shone in the dark sky. Again the old lady disappeared and returned in the morning with another strange story. This time, however, her husband sat up and took an interest.

'Last night we met in Maisy's cottage. We each stood by the hearth and one by one we put a foot on the crook of the hook that held the cooking pot. We said the magic words we learned from the fairies of Lapland and whoosh! One by one we were up the chimney like puffs of smoke. We flew over the Firth of Forth, across the Pentland Hills and on and on until we were at the Bishop's Palace at Carlisle.'

'Well I never!' exclaimed her husband. 'Did you go inside?'

'Indeed we did, for all the bolts on the doors flew open and there we were, down in the wine cellars. We tasted his fine wine and then quick as a wink we flew back to Fife, safe at home and all before the cockerel crowed.'

'This is wonderful!' said the old man, jumping up. He took off his nightcap and rubbed his ears. 'What an amazing wife I have! Tell me the magic words and I shall visit the Bishop's cellars myself.'

But the guidwife shook her head, 'I cannot!' she said. 'Imagine what would happen if I told you and you told someone else. Soon the whole world would be upside down and people would be flying all over the place into other folks' homes and up to all sorts of mischief. Then there would be trouble.'

Try as he might, the old man could not discover the magic words so he decided to use trickery. When the next new moon appeared he sneaked out of the house and went to the cottage out on the moor. He hid behind a big kist and waited. Just as his old bones began to ache, the door opened. In trooped his wife and the other witches.

'Where shall we go tonight?' she asked. 'The wind is cold and I have a fancy to try more of those fine wines in the Bishop's cellar.'

'Agreed!' laughed the others, and one by one they went to the fireplace.

The old man peeped above the kist and saw the first witch step on to a stool. Then she put her foot on to the crook of the hook that held the cooking pot, said the magic words, and was whisked up the chimney. As fast as she had disappeared, another of the women took her place. Five times the old man heard the magic words and five times he watched the women disappear.

'I can do it too!' he chuckled gleefully, and came out from his hiding place.

He stepped on the stool, put his foot on the crook of the hook and repeated the magic words. He was away up the chimney before he had time to blink!

The witches flew through the air and behind them flew the old man. They flew over the Firth of Forth and through the clouds above the Pentland Hills. In the distance the old man saw the Bishop's Palace and then, just as his wife had said, the doors flew open. It was not until they landed in the Bishop's cellar that the witches discovered the old man had also flown

with them. He had tricked them! But there was nothing to be done so the women began to enjoy themselves, taking a little wine from one cask and a little wine from another.

'See, Husband,' said the old woman, 'we do little harm and the Bishop will not notice this tiny amount of his wine has gone.'

But the old man was not so wise. Instead of a little sip here and a small taste there he filled his goblet at each barrel and soon he was singing the bonny songs of Fife. However, before too long he was feeling drowsy and he leaned against a huge barrel and fell fast asleep on the damp floor. That is where his wife and her friends left him when it was time to leave.

The guidman slept, snoring and dreaming until well into the day when five of the Bishop's servants tripped over him in the dark cellar. Of course, they wanted to know who he was and how he got in through a locked door. The old man could not speak and his head was so muddled by the wine he could not think. Finally he told them, 'I am a guidman from Fife and I flew on the wind with my wife.'

Well they thought he must be a wizard so they dragged him outside and the old man's head soon cleared itself with pure fright. The guards took him into the courtyard where a crowd had gathered.

'Dearie, dearie me! I wish I had stayed in bed,' he said to himself as they put a great chain round his waist and piled up logs of wood round his feet. They lit a fire.

'Oh dearie me, what will my poor wife say?' he wondered, as the smoke began to curl upwards.

At that very moment a great grey bird swooped down out of the sky carrying something red in its claw. There was a flutter of wings and a swish of feathers as the bird settled on the old man's shoulders, placing his red nightcap on his head. The grey bird croaked into the guidman's ear and he let out an enormous shout of joy, 'My wife! My guidwife!'

Indeed, it was the old lady in the form of the grey bird, sitting on his shoulder. After she croaked the magic words into his ear she flew off over the palace walls.

The old man looked into the flames and repeated the magic words in a whisper, 'Deliver me please from strife … send me home safe to Fife!'

The chains fell off and he pulled his red nightcap down firmly over his head and jumped upwards. The crowd watched the old man fly over the palace walls and his laughter could be heard long after he reached the clouds in the sky. He flew faster than the wind until he reached his own wee house, safe in the Kingdom of Fife.

Some time passed, but one night when a bright new moon crept above the trees the guidwife put on her cape and her bonnet and stepped outside. The old man reached for his red nightcap and I'm sure you know where he went!

The Water Horse of Loch Garve

HIGHLANDS

Many long years ago the Each Uisge, the water horse of Loch Garve, took a wife. She loved the beautiful mountains and hills surrounding the clear waters that were filled with gleaming fish. She loved swimming with her husband and snatching fish from the fishing lines of frustrated fishermen. She loved her watery home during summer. But when the seasons changed the waters became very cold and the poor wife complained. Once it was winter and the waters froze the poor wife wept and complained even more. The water horse loved his wife but he didn't know what he could do to make her happy.

One cold, windy day as he was swimming close by the little village of Garve he looked at the cottages. He saw smoke coming from the chimneys and knew that inside the families were cosy and warm. Then he had an idea! He looked across the loch to where a cottage stood alone, sheltered by the mountain. A builder lived there and he was at home, for smoke rose from the chimney.

The water horse dived down deep and began to swim faster and faster, heading for the bank of the loch.

Suddenly a huge wave of water hit the shore and out of the spray stepped a great black stallion.

The water horse pranced up to the door of the cottage and he stomped his foot three times. The builder looked through the window wondering who could be calling on him. He saw the black stallion, water dripping from his mane and tail, and he knew this was the Each Uisge. The water horse snorted and stomped again and the man knew he must answer the door.

The builder stood unafraid, listening to the water horse explain his problem. He saw how much the water horse loved his poor wife and for some long time the two discussed how to resolve the situation. The builder told him that he would need help, for the task was not easy, and the black stallion readily agreed, on one condition.

'I will wear no bridle or bit in my mouth,' he said, and the builder understood he did not want to be trapped.

'Will you promise to return me to my home safe and sound?' asked the builder, who knew the stories of people taken to a watery death by water horses.

'I will do you no harm,' the water horse replied, 'and what payment do you want for the work?'

'Well you can promise not to take the fish from my fishing line in future!' laughed the builder.

In the days that followed, people on the other side of the loch peered through the mists and sometimes caught a glimpse of a great black stallion hauling stones for the builder. No one knew he had a horse and no one knew of a black stallion in Sutherland. One or two people thought of the legend of the water horse but no one spoke of it.

Finally all was ready and the water horse asked the builder to sit on his back. This was the real test of trust. Mounting a water horse was a dangerous thing to do. But the Each Uisge had asked a favour and made a promise and the builder looked into his dark eyes and mounted without fear.

The builder and the water horse took all the stones to the depths of the loch and eventually the job was done. He had built a fireplace and a chimney and at last the poor wife was warm, and the water horse was happy.

In all the years that followed the builder never had a fish snatched from his line, much to the frustration of the other fishermen. When times were hard he found fish on his doorstep. Just one or twice people saw a great black stallion hauling stones for the builder.

That part of Loch Garve never freezes of course and now you know why!

The Orra Man

LANARKSHIRE

Once there lived an orra man, an odd-job man, who worked on a farm in Lanarkshire. He did whatever jobs he was offered and he worked hard in order to look after his wife and two small children.

One day the farmer asked the orra man to go to the moorland near Merlin's Crag to cut peats and to lay them out to dry, ready to store for winter. So he set off towards the steep, rugged rock that folk believed was once the home of Merlin, the great magician.

The orra man began to work as soon as he arrived. He dug into the peat bank with his special peat-cutting spade and made neat blocks of thick turf and stacked each one to dry. He worked so hard that before too long he had dug his way close to the crag.

Suddenly he stopped.

There was a tiny woman right by his feet. She was the smallest woman he had seen in all his life, standing no taller than his own wee toddling baby. She wore a green gown and red stockings but she did not wear a hat or a ribbon and her long, yellow hair was loose about her shoulders.

The orra man stopped his work and leant on his spade, gazing in wonder at the little lady. He was even more surprised when she pointed a tiny finger and spoke to him.

'How would you like it if I sent my husband round to take the roof off your house?' she said crossly. 'You mortals think you can do anything you like.'

The poor man didn't move. He just stared in amazement until she stamped her tiny foot saying, 'You have dug up the roof of our house; now put it back instantly, or you shall regret this day.'

The orra man was truly frightened. He knew the wee folk might cause great harm to men who offended them and so, without another thought, he set to work. He lifted each square of turf and very carefully put each one back into the exact spot from which he'd dug it out. He was very tired when he had finished and he looked over his shoulder to see if the tiny lady was pleased.

She had vanished completely. He looked all around but he could not see where she might have gone.

But now he had another problem – the farmer! He lifted his spade over his shoulder and trudged towards the farm and, of course, the farmer saw him coming home early and wanted to know if the job had been completed.

The poor man stuttered and his hands were shaking as he explained about the wee woman.

The farmer laughed but the orra man told him how angry the wee lady had been and how he had replaced her roof and the peats he had dug up.

'I did not want her to bring bad luck to your farm,' he explained.

The farmer laughed even more, 'I do not believe in ghosts or brownies or the wee folk. Things you cannot see do not bring you harm!'

'But I did see her!' cried the poor man wringing his hands in fear, 'Let me dig for peats in another place.'

The farmer was cross, 'This is just a silly superstition and I will cure your fear. Take the horse and cart now. Go and dig up the peat and bring it back to the farm to dry out. By the time you have finished you will see I am right.'

So the orra man had to return to his work, but with a heavy heart. He lifted all the peats he had so carefully replaced and loaded them on to the cart, all the while keeping a lookout for the wee lady.

He took the peat back to the farm.

'So where is your wee lady?' laughed the farmer.

The weary man shrugged his shoulders as he stacked the peat to dry. There was no trouble at the farm all winter.

Spring arrived and the orra man helped the farmer with the ploughing and sowing the crops. He helped with the sheep and the new lambs. There were many odd jobs to do and he worked hard. He thought of the wee lady but there was no trouble at the farm all spring.

Then summer arrived and the orra man was very busy. He took vegetables to market and thatched the byres. He milked the cows and mended fences. He helped with the haymaking. Sometimes he thought about the tiny woman.

'Maybe I did imagine the wee lady in her red stockings,' said the orra man to himself. There was no trouble at the farm all summer.

Autumn arrived and the orra man was very busy indeed. There was the harvesting of wheat, and potatoes and turnips to dig. He worked so hard he had no time to think of the wee lady. Then one day, exactly one year after seeing the wee lady, he saw the farmer who called out to him.

'I am very pleased with your hard work so finish up early today and take this can of milk home to your wife as a little present,' said the farmer.

The sun was shining as the happy man set off towards his cottage. He was humming a tune to himself as he passed close by the foot of Merlin's Crag. Suddenly he felt very tired. His feet felt as heavy as lead and it seemed such a long way down the road before he would get home.

'I will have to sit and rest a bit,' thought the poor man, yawning, 'I have been working hard since sunrise and I cannot keep my eyes open.'

He set the pail of milk down in the shade of Merlin's Crag and sat on the soft grass without thinking just where he was and soon he had fallen fast asleep.

When he did wake up it was almost midnight and the moon had risen above the crag, casting an eerie silver light. The orra man thought he saw tiny figures so he rubbed his eyes and peered into the pale shadows. There they were again. A whole band of the wee folk dancing round and round him, singing and laughing. They pointed their tiny fingers at him and shook their little fists.

'I must get home,' said the orra man and stood up.

He tried to walk away but in vain. No matter which way he turned or how fast he stepped out he could not leave the circle of wee folk that went whichever way he did. He could not escape. He was trapped in a magic fairy ring!

'Why do you want to leave us, man?' called out the prettiest wee lass. 'Come dance with me and you will not be in such a hurry to go.'

The orra man shook his head because he knew little of dancing.

'I have clumsy feet,' he said, but the wee lass reached up and took his hands.

Suddenly he was no longer tired. He skipped and waltzed and whirled around as if he had been a dancer all his life.

'I could dance like this all night,' he laughed as he forgot all his worries.

He forgot the pail of milk and his wife and his little children waiting at home. He forgot everything except how happy he was dancing with the wee folk.

All night they danced and sang and laughed until the first pale light of day crept over the moorland. The farmyard cockerel crowed to greet the dawn.

Instantly the laughter and dancing stopped.

'Quick, we must away!' they called to each other. 'The sun is rising! Run, run!'

The wee folk closed round the startled man and pushed and shoved at him until he was running as fast as he could. They rushed towards the crag.

He saw a secret door open into the very rock face and before he could even think, the wee folk had swept him along inside.

He was in a large hall where all around him the wee folk went to rest on their tiny couches, tired after all their dancing. The orra man was tired too so he found a corner out of the way and sat down and though he was so large, there was plenty of room. Soon he fell asleep.

When he woke he wondered what would happen next but he just sat, happy to watch the wee ones going about their secret chores. He saw many mysterious things. They were busy around his large feet as if he was not even there. They did not speak to him and he did not try to talk to them. He did not even think of escaping. He sat until he felt someone touch his shoulder.

It was the little woman who had spoken to him a year ago! She still wore the green dress and the red stockings and her long, yellow hair was spread about her shoulders as before.

'I have come to tell you that the turf that you took from the roof of my house has grown once more,' she said, amused by the man's blank stare.

'What do you mean?' he asked her. 'It takes years to grow back.'

'That's right,' she said. 'You have been here long enough for the grass to grow back over the ground you once dug up,' and she held out a tiny hand to him.

'Come. You have been punished for long enough and it is time for you to return to your home.'

He got up and stretched his aching legs. It would be nice to go home he thought but he stopped as the wee lady pointed her tiny finger at him once again.

'Remember us man, but promise never to tell a mortal being what you have seen here!' she commanded.

The man swore he would not betray them and suddenly he found himself at the foot of Merlin's Crag in the bright sunshine and the wee lady was nowhere to be seen. He picked up the pail of milk that was still quite fresh and continued down the road towards his cottage.

'Good Morning!' he greeted his neighbours, who were setting about their early morning chores. Some of them turned away as if he was a stranger but others looked at him as if he was a ghost.

When he reached his own cottage he stood at the gate and stared. His wee bairns were now tall, strong children. His wife looked at him as if he had returned from the dead.

'I've brought you some milk,' he managed to say.

'Milk!' the poor woman cried. 'After seven long years you have brought us some milk! How could you leave us like that?"

The orra man put down the pail of milk and looked back up the road. The wee folk had indeed punished him. He had taken the roof from their home and for seven years while their home was ruined his own family had suffered. All of them had suffered.

He looked up at Merlin's Crag standing tall in the moorland and vowed never to walk that road again.

The orra man was happy to be safe at home, but late at night, as the years went by, he thought of the wee folk. He often thought of the little lady in her green dress and red stockings and he hoped she and her family were as happy as he was and that no other mortal had disturbed their fairy homeland.

Tam Lin

BORDERS

Oh I forbid you, maidens a',
That wear gowd about your hair,
To come or gae by Carterhaugh,
For young Tam Lin is there.

Child's Ballads

Once, in Ettrickdale there lived a young boy,
Tam Lin. For hundreds of years folk have sung
the ballad, but I shall *tell* you the story.

As a young boy Tam Lin went to live with his
grandfather, the Duke of Roxburgh, and when
he was old enough he was given a beautiful
white pony and his grandfather taught him
how to hunt. One day they set off through the

Forest of Carterhaugh, Tam Lin on his white pony with all the huntsmen and the dogs running ahead. It was so noisy, so exciting, and the horses ran so fast that no one noticed when Tam Lin fell from his steed. But the Queen of the Fairies was watching and she stole Tam Lin for herself.

No matter how much they searched that forest they could not find Tam Lin and so the stories grew over the following years. Was he a mortal man or was he a fairy? Had the Queen of Fairies cast a spell over him? Some folk said he demanded a ransom for safe passage through the forest and others said he did not exist at all.

Now the Forest of Carterhaugh belonged to young Lady Janet who lived in a castle nearby. Every time she looked across the fields to the forest she wondered about Tam Lin and so early one morning she brushed her golden hair and, wearing a gown of green, set off alone to see if she could find him.

The forest was dark and there were no paths and so she called his name, 'Tam Lin? Tam Lin?' On and on she wandered until she came to a clearing and there was a well and beside the well stood a white pony. There were roses growing close by and she picked one and instantly knew that someone stood behind her.

When she turned she saw a young man with the saddest grey eyes you could imagine.

'Why do you take my rose Janet? What brings you here without my permission?' he asked.

Janet knew it must be Tam Lin and she replied, 'I do not need your permission to come or go from Carterhaugh for my daddy gave me this forest. It is mine.'

'Ah Janet, what you and your father do not know is that this forest belongs to the Queen of Fairies and you should leave. If she found you here I do not know what she would do,' said Tam Lin. 'I shall lead you safely to the edge of the forest and you should return home and forget me.'

But she could not forget Tam Lin and every time she looked across the fields to the forest she wondered if he was happy there or whether he might want to leave. Janet and her ladies played ball in the sunshine and chess in the evenings while summer turned to autumn and the leaves on the trees turned to red and gold.

One day an old knight offered to marry Janet and while her father thought this was a good idea she did not! There was only one person she would marry and so on the very last day of October she set off for Carterhaugh.

This time it was as if her feet knew where to go and soon she reached the clearing and, as before, the white pony stood beside the well. Only two roses remained on the bush and as she picked one Tam Lin called out, 'Why have you returned Janet?'

'I have to know if you are an earthly man or if you are a fairy and I want to know if you want to leave this forest with me?' she said.

Tam Lin told her the story of how he was indeed a mortal man, lost as a child and stolen by the Queen of the Fairies. 'And while I would come with you, Janet, I may not, for the queen has made me Guardian of this forest and here I must stay.'

'But surely there is some way to break the spell?' Janet asked him.

He sighed, 'Maybe on this night, Hallowe'en, the spell could be broken for tonight the Queen of the Fairies and all the fairy folk ride out to pay their dues to the devil with a mortal man. I fear this year it might be me.'

'What can I do?' Janet asked.

'At midnight the fairy folk will ride out to Miles Cross by the town. The queen will be on her great black stallion, the king will ride a fine brown horse and I will be riding my milk-white steed. You must pull me down from the pony and hold me in your arms no matter what happens. The Queen of the Fairies will change me into all kinds of beasts. Hold me fast. Even when you feel I am a burning brand of iron, do not let go but once I am changed into a burning torch throw me into the well. Wear a green cloak Janet and wrap me in this and then I will be saved.'

'I will be there,' said Janet

Late that night Janet wrapped herself in her warm green cloak and walked to Miles Cross at the edge of the town. An owl hooted softly and a fox stepped across her path. The north wind carried strange sounds and Janet shivered as she hid behind the ancient stone cross.

Then she saw a shimmer of lights from fairy lanterns and she heard the jingle of tiny bells. The procession passed her. First came the queen on her prancing black stallion and then came the king on his proud brown horse. The third horse was milk-white and Janet wasted not a moment. She jumped up and dragged Tam Lin from the saddle. They tumbled on to the ground and she hung on to him for dear life.

All around, the fairies ran screeching and screaming and suddenly Janet felt herself being crushed. It was a great silver python wrapping itself around her and she tried to push it off when she remembered what Tam Lin had said and so she closed her eyes and hung on to that snake for dear life.

The Queen of the Fairies hissed in anger and suddenly Janet felt herself lifted high in the air and she was holding on to the fur of a great brown bear. It growled and she nearly let go but she remembered what Tam Lin had said so she hung on to that bear for dear life.

Poor Janet felt herself dashed to the ground and her fingers were tangled in long, matted hair and a hot, foul-stinking breath hit her in the face. She opened her eyes and she was staring into the jaws of a lion. She nearly let go but she remembered what Tam Lin had said and so she shut her eyes and hung on to that lion for dear life.

Then she screamed. In her hands was a bar of red-hot iron and she knew she could not hold it. The tears ran down her cheeks and the Queen of the Fairies laughed but Janet remembered what Tam Lin had said and she cried out, 'I love you Tam Lin,' and she hung on to that red-hot iron for dear life.

Suddenly the fairies were still. In Janet's hands was a bright, burning torch. She remembered what Tam Lin had said and she ran to the well and threw the torch into the water and the steam hissed up and out of the steam stepped Tam Lin.

Quick as a flash she wrapped her green cloak around him and he was safe.

The Queen of the Fairies went white with rage, 'You! You have stolen my bonniest knight,' she said to Janet and then she turned on Tam Lin. 'Had I known, I would have taken out your heart and given you one of stone!'

Just then the sun peeped over the hill and the cockerel crowed. The fairies were gone and Tam Lin looked down at Janet. 'You are a brave wee lassie Janet and you have saved my life. If you would have me I will be yours for evermore.'

Janet smiled, 'I will have you Tam Lin just so long as I never have to hug another snake, another bear, or another lion!'

And she never did.

The Changeling of Kintalen

ARGYLLSHIRE

In Kintalen, a long time ago, there was a mother who had a new baby son. At first all was well but after a couple of weeks the baby started crying. He cried all day and most of the night and no matter how much she fed the baby, kept him dry and rocked the cradle the baby cried.

The poor mother was so tired but she was also worried for, in spite of all the feeding, the baby did not grow as strong and healthy as other babies in the village. There was no one to help because no one wanted to spend time with a baby that screamed and cried for no good reason at all. It seemed this baby would not let its poor mother out of sight. When it came to harvest time she could not take her sickle and join the others in the fields.

Now all that long time ago people spun wool and wove their own cloth but travelling tailors would come to the villages to sew clothes. And so one day a tailor came to the mother's house to do some sewing for her. Of course the baby was crying but that did not worry the tailor, in fact he was quite suspicious about this baby for he had heard it wailing ever since he'd arrived in the village.

'You go and join the harvesting,' he said to the mother, 'I'll look after the baby.'

No sooner was the poor mother out of the door than the baby started to scream. The tailor went to the cradle and there he saw a strange sight for the baby was quite wizened and wrinkled. The wise tailor felt sure this must be a changeling, a fairy child, left behind when the fairies had stolen the mother's own baby. The baby looked at him and wailed even louder.

'Oh stop that music lad or I shall sit you on the fire,' said the tailor, knowing full well that a real baby would not understand those words at all.

The changeling stopped crying for a while and the tailor got on with his sewing. But when the screeching started again the tailor called out, 'You only sing one tune my lad and I do not like it. If you will not stop I will kill you with my dirk!' The changeling was quiet for some time.

The tailor began to hum a tune as he stitched and suddenly the changeling set up such a howl that the tailor jumped up and went over to the cradle.

'We have all had enough of this music of yours!' he said crossly. 'Now here is my dirk and I shall cut your throat unless you find your bagpipes and play me a real tune.'

The changeling sat up in the cradle, took the pipes that he had kept hidden, and struck up the sweetest music the tailor had ever heard.

The people harvesting in the field heard the music, dropped their sickles and stood listening. Some even ran back to the village to see this wonderful piper, but before they got there the tune had stopped and so they returned to the harvesting.

In the evening the tailor watched for the villagers coming home and he went out to meet the baby's mother. There was no screeching and wailing coming from the house and she was astonished. The tailor told her all that had happened and she could hardly believe her ears.

'But what should I do and how will I get my own baby back?' she wanted to know.

'Take the changeling to the loch and throw him in,' said the tailor, 'and remember it is not a real baby, just a changeling. I will come with you.'

As soon as the mother entered the house the changeling began crying and screaming hoping to be fed some dinner. But the mother picked it up and went down to the loch with the tailor and threw it into the water.

Instantly the changeling became a grey-haired old man and swam to the other side of Loch Sween. When he got to dry land, he shouted and waved his fists at her but she and the tailor were too far away to hear what he said.

She returned home and heard a little whimper from the cradle. There she found her own baby safe and sound and with the happiest of hearts she sat the baby on her hip and prepared a fine supper, the finest the tailor had ever eaten.

Old Croovie

ABERDEENSHIRE

Jack was a kind and honest lad but his master, the Laird of the Black Arts, was as cruel as he was mean. Jack looked after the laird's sheep from dawn to dusk and all for two pennies a week. In spite of the poor pay, Jack was happy with his job for he liked nothing better than to be outside in the fields and the woods all day. He knew every tree and bush and all the ferns and wildflowers that grew on the laird's estate.

Jack lived with his mother in a wee tumbledown cottage and every day she would bring Jack his lunch and if it was not raining she would sit with him, spinning the clumps of wool she found on bushes and fences.

One Midsummer's Eve, Jack was on the hill watching the sheep in a field above the Old

Lumphinan Road. That part of the road was lined with oak trees and the greatest and oldest of these was known as Old Croovie. On the other side of the road were birch trees and the land fell away to a stream. It was a lovely day: the sheep were bleating, the birds were singing and the bees were buzzing. But suddenly all the birds gathered on the branches of Old Croovie took flight, screeching and crying, and Jack heard them calling, 'We're off, we're off! Tonight's the night! We're off!'

Well, Jack wondered what that meant and so when his mother arrived with his piece he told her what he'd seen and heard.

'Folk in these parts say that once in each hundred years, Old Croovie and his pals lift themselves out of the earth to dance with the birch trees,' said his mother. 'I guess the birds know tonight must be the night.'

'Well,' said Jack, 'That would be a rare thing to see. I will stay and watch.'

His mother was worried, 'Do be careful Jack, for I fear there is great danger around on nights like tonight.' She took a ball of blue wool she'd been spinning and thrust it into Jack's hands. "Take this, Jack, you might need it, and do remember: no good ever comes to the greedy!'

And off she went back home while Jack sat wondering what possible use he might have for a ball of his mother's homespun wool. Soon after, Jack's sweetheart, Jeannie, came running up the hill. She worked as a maid in the big house and arrived all out of breath.

'What's the matter?' asked Jack

'Tis the Laird of the Black Arts!' she said. 'He's in such a peculiar state. He's got some wild notion about Old Croovie and has forbidden any of the servants to leave the house after dusk.'

That made Jack even more determined to stay to see what would happen. Jeannie warned him to take care and then she ran back to the house.

Of course it hardly gets dark at all in Aberdeenshire at midsummer but in those twilight hours around midnight after the moon had appeared above the horizon, Jack woke suddenly from a doze. He heard soft music, a sweet harp-like tune all around him.

'The music got louder and the birch trees on the other side of the road began to sway and then to Jack's amazement they lifted themselves right out of the ground and waltzed down the slope towards the stream.

Meanwhile, Old Croovie and the other oaks were stretching their branches and then with a great tearing sound they heaved their massive bodies out of the ground leaving great gaping root holes behind.

Old Croovie led the oaks to join the dance. Jack watched entranced as each oak tree grasped a birch tree and they birled around faster and faster as the music got louder and wilder.

Then he saw the Laird of the Black Arts come striding down from the big house.

'Be gone with you lad!' said the laird as soon as he saw Jack. 'You have no business here tonight. Go home or I'll have you arrested for poaching.'

Jack had no intention of leaving and instead he hid behind a bush and watched as the laird went down into the biggest root hole, the very place where Old Croovie had stood for hundreds of years.

Jack crept over to a smaller hole nearest to him and peered inside. When his eyes adjusted to the darkness he was astounded to see gold goblets, silver rings, jewel-encrusted bracelets and many other treasures lying at the bottom of the hole.

He climbed down into the hole and looked all around. Remembering his mother's words, he did not stuff his pockets full but he couldn't resist taking a pretty little silver cup for his

mother and a beautiful gold ring for Jeannie. He took a small handful of jewels for himself and then began to climb out of the hole, but every time he tried to get a grip the sides crumbled away. He was trapped.

You can imagine how relieved he was to see Jeannie's head pop over the edge of the hole.

'Jack, Jack you must hurry,' she cried, 'the music is slowing down and I think the dance will soon end.'

Jack took the ball of his mother's spun wool, held one end fast and threw the ball up to Jeannie. She held on tightly, the wool was strong – spun with his mother's love – and Jack was nimble and soon he was out of that hole.

Jack and Jeannie ran as fast as they could to Old Croovie's root hole where the greedy laird was stuffing a huge sack full of gold and many treasures.

'Come out quickly,' called Jack to his master, 'the dance is over and Old Croovie is coming back.'

'Be off!' said the laird without looking up, 'you'll take a drop in wages for your disob …!'

It was too late, Old Croovie was already standing over the spot and with a great sigh of exhaustion he settled back down into his root hole, burying both treasure and the Laird of the Black Arts, who was of course never seen again.

Jack gave his mother the silver cup, and Jeannie the gold ring. By and by Jack and Jeannie were married and with his handful of jewels he was able to build a bigger and better cottage, which they shared with Jack's mother.

The laird's son inherited the estate and he was a kindly master, and not quite as mean as his father, increasing his faithful shepherd's wage to two and a half pennies a week.

I heard this story from the great storyteller Stanley Robertson as we stood on the Old Lumphinan Road, under the branches of Old Croovie. Maybe you too will see this magical tree one day, if you happen to pass that way.

The Midwife's Tale

LOTHIAN

Once upon a time in Edinburgh there lived a woman who was a midwife and she was well loved, for it was she who helped all the babies to be born. At this time the city was bounded by a great wall and each night the gates were locked to keep the citizens safely enclosed. The midwife and her husband lived in a few small rooms in one of the tall buildings down a narrow wynd.

One dark night when all were sound asleep there was a loud knocking at the door. She jumped up and peered through the window, but all she could see was the dark figure of a man holding a lantern.

'Would you come with me please? We have a baby on the way and the mother needs your help,' the man called out.

The midwife got dressed as fast as she could, rushed down the stairs and followed the light of the lantern, although she could not see the person who was carrying it. They went up the wynd and out on to the High Street and finally arrived at the Netherbow Gates. The midwife was amazed to see the gates open as if by magic and, although she was worried, she quickly followed the lantern bearer out of the city. They went down the Canongate and into the dark woods that in those days surrounded Holyrood Abbey.

Finally the light stopped moving. Between the roots of a large tree a hidden trapdoor opened and she saw steep steps leading underground. With trembling knees the midwife followed her mysterious guide, and before long she found herself in a roomy chamber surrounded by wee folk.

'Welcome, midwife,' they said, 'we need your help tonight.'

One of the wee ladies showed her into a room and there she saw a little woman who took her by the hand.

'Stay with me and make sure my baby is born healthy and strong. As soon as it is born you must rub some of this ointment on to each eyelid,' she said, giving the midwife a tiny jar of ointment.

The midwife sat with the woman and before morning a tiny baby was born, healthy and strong. The midwife did as she was told and put some ointment on the baby's eyelids. She was just about to put the lid back on the jar when she had a thought. If this was good for the wee folk then it might be good for her. So she rubbed some ointment onto her right eyelid. Nothing happened. She almost put some ointment on to her left eyelid but at the last moment she changed her mind.

Since mother and child were both doing well, the midwife asked to be taken home. But the wee folk did not want to let her go.

'Stay with us for a while and let us reward you,' they said.

The wee folk often went out, returning with all kinds of pretty things – lace, ribbons, trinkets and jewels. Each day they treated her better than the day before, giving her many little presents and fine food. But the only thing she wanted was to go home.

Finally after eight days the wee folk agreed to let her go home, but only after she had swept the floor. It was an odd request but she did as she was asked and just as she piled up the dust they told her, 'For your reward you may take those sweepings!'

The midwife was smart enough to not despise the unusual gift and so she brushed the sweepings into her apron. Then, as it was dark, she followed the man with his lantern as she had done before and soon she arrived safely at home, much to the amazement of her husband, who had been terribly worried. She told him everything that had happened and when he asked about her payment the midwife shook the sweepings out of her apron on to the table before him. What a surprise! There on the table was a pile of shining gold pieces!

The next day the midwife, who was very pleased to have some money, went up the High Street to the Lawn Market to walk among the stalls filled with linen, lace and many fine goods. Suddenly she saw the wee folk scattered throughout the crowd. The midwife was shocked to see they were stealing from the stalls but that the stallholders clearly could not see them. Without thinking she called out, 'Hey! What are you doing?'

The wee folk recognised her but were surprised and angry.

'You can see us? How?' they demanded.

She covered her right eye and she could not see them at all with just her left eye. She realised then that she could see them only with her right eye, the eye she had rubbed with the fairy's ointment. She covered her left eye, 'I see you with my right eye.'

Without warning the wee folk blew into her right eye, and in that instant the eye was blinded. She never saw the wee folk again.

However, she had thought quickly and had protected her left eye and so she was able to live long and happy with all her riches. And if she ever noticed a linen handkerchief or a piece of lace slipping off a market stall she was wise enough to say nothing.

The Tailor of Saddell Castle

ARGYLLSHIRE

Long ago there lived the great Laird MacDonald who was so rich that he could employ a tailor to work year round at his castle at Saddell, on the east coast of Kintyre. One day he called for the tailor because he wanted a new pair of trews.

'That'll be soon enough done,' said the tailor.

But MacDonald also made a strange request. He wanted the trews to be made at night in the old ruined abbey.

'For I hear the abbey is haunted by a fearsome thing seen only at dead of night. I will pay you for the trews but double the reward for the story you bring back.'

So the tailor agreed and he cut the fabric and put together his needles and thread and when night came the tailor set off up the glen to the ruined abbey, about half a mile from the castle. Inside he found a gravestone to serve as a seat and he lit his candle, put on his thimble and set to work on the trews, stitching and sewing, his needle shining, and all the while thinking of the handsome reward he'd collect from MacDonald.

He was doing quite well when all of a sudden he felt the ground tremble under his feet. Keeping his fingers at work he looked about him and spied a great head rising up through the stone floor of the abbey.

'Do you see this great head of mine?' the thing said.

'I see that, but I'll sew this!' replied the tailor, stitching and sewing.

Then the head rose higher, higher, through the stone floor until its neck appeared.

'Do you see this great neck of mine?'

'I see that, but I'll sew this!' replied the tailor as he stitched and sewed, stitched and sewed.

The thing rose even higher still until great shoulders and a chest appeared above the ground.

'Do you see this great chest of mine?'

Again the tailor replied, 'I see that, but I'll sew this!'

Still it kept rising above the stone floor until it shook a great pair of arms in the tailor's face, 'Do you see these great arms of mine?'

'I see that, but I'll sew this!' and he stitched faster and faster for he knew he had no time to lose. He began to sew with longer stitches as he watched it rising, rising until it lifted out a leg and stamped it on the floor.

It roared, 'Do you see this great leg of mine?'

'Aye, aye, I see that, but I'll sew this!' cried the tailor. His fingers flew with the needle and the stitches got longer and longer. He had almost finished the trews when the thing began lifting its other leg. But before the thing could pull its other leg above the stone floor, the tailor finished the trews. He blew out the candle, bundled up the trews under his arm, jumped off the gravestone and ran out of the abbey.

The fearsome thing gave a great howl, stamped with both its feet on the stone floor and out of the abbey it went after the tailor. Down the glen they ran, but the tailor had a head start, a nimble pair of legs and no wish to lose the laird's reward. He ran and the thing ran, he ran and it ran, faster and faster.

The thing howled again but the tailor held the trews tight and let no darkness grow under his feet until he reached Saddell Castle. No sooner was he inside and the door slammed shut than the thing was upon it grasping at the stone doorjamb with great fury.

The noise woke all within the castle and they rushed down the stairs to find the tailor, white as a sheet and panting hard. He gave the trews to the laird. MacDonald never noticed some of the stitches were somewhat long

because he was so interested in the story the tailor had to tell and for this he more than doubled the reward!

If you ever visit Saddell Castle, look closely at the stone doorjamb and there you will see the five finger marks left by the fearsome thing.

The Poor Widow's Son and the Stranger

LOWLANDS

Once there was a widow who had a number of children and they were so poor they barely had enough clothes to share, and even less food. One night when the children were crying with hunger the widow could think of no way to get them quietly to bed. Finally she had an idea and taking the cooking pot out to the well she filled it with water and into the water she added a large round stone.

'Now here's a fine lump of meat,' she told them when she came back in, 'so if you all go to sleep now I'll make soup and it will be ready when you wake up.' She hung the pot over the fire and began to stir and one by one the hungry children fell asleep, even her oldest, a son.

A little later there was a knock at the door and when she opened it there stood a stranger.

'I've travelled a long way and I have a long way yet to travel. May I stay the night?' he said.

'This is a poor house and I have no food to offer you,' she replied, ashamed because she had nothing to share with the weary traveller, 'but you are welcome to sleep here tonight.'

'Tell me then, what are you cooking in the pot over the fire?' he asked her.

'It's only a stone,' she told him, 'a trick to send the children to sleep.'

The stranger walked over, peered into the pot and called her to come and look.

'Why, this is an excellent piece of beef,' he said, and to her great surprise that's just what he pulled out of the pot.

She rubbed her eyes and could not believe what she was seeing. The stranger spoke again, 'Go to the chest and bring out plenty of bread, some butter and whatever else you think should go into the pot.'

She did as he said even though she knew the chest was empty. However, when she opened it up there, to her amazement, she found bread, butter, milk and plenty of vegetables to add to the pot.

When the soup was ready she woke the children. They had never seen so much food

and after every one of them had eaten all they could the oldest son begged the stranger for a story. The stranger was happy to tell a story, for every traveller has a tale to tell.

When it was ended he turned to the young lad, 'Now you have the story what will you give me in return?'

'I have nothing to give,' replied the lad.

The stranger took him outside and turned him into a snake, letting him loose in the long grass, 'At the end of seven days you must tell me what you will give,' he told the snake.

After seven days the stranger returned and asked again, 'What will you give in return for the story I gave you?'

'I have nothing to give,' replied the snake.

So the stranger took the snake, turned it into a deer and said, 'At the end of seven days you must tell me what you will give for my story.'

For seven days the deer ran in the woods and when the stranger returned he asked again, 'Have you thought what you will give for the story I gave you?'

'I have nothing to give,' replied the deer.

The stranger turned the deer into an eagle and said, 'At the end of seven days you must tell me what you will give and this will be your last chance.'

The eagle flew off, over the forest and over the mountains.

But at the end of these seven days he was waiting when the stranger asked for the last time, 'What will you give me for my story?'

This time he received a different answer.

'I have nothing to give except for my thanks,' said the eagle and instantly was turned back into the poor widow's son.

'If you had said this the first time,' said the stranger, 'you would have saved both of us a great deal of trouble. Now let me tell you how you might change your family's fortune forever.

Have you heard of an old castle that's kept by a giant?'

The poor widow's son knew of the castle. 'People say it is enchanted,' he told the stranger.

'Well if you truly want to seek your fortune that is where you must go,' said the stranger. 'When you arrive you will find the guards sleeping, for everyone there is under a spell. Go through all the rooms until you find the King of Scotland's daughter asleep on a marble table. Above her head hangs a sword that you must touch but do not take it down for that will only bring you bad luck. The princess will wake for a short time and she will tell you what you must do to save her and all those under the sleeping spell.'

The stranger left and the poor widow's son set off. Because he had lived as a snake he travelled silently and because he had lived as a deer he ran swiftly. He knew just where to go because as an eagle he had flown over the castle. He travelled and he travelled until at last he reached the silent castle. The giant was nowhere to be seen and inside everything was just as he'd been told. The guards were asleep and sleeping on a marble table he found the king's daughter. He touched the sword and she woke up amazed that anyone had been able to enter the giant's castle without being seen.

'I saw no giant,' he told her.

'Then beware,' she said, 'for he will return to the castle shortly to stand guard outside.'

'If I am to save you and the others in this castle what must I do?' he asked her.

'You must slay the giant. But that cannot be done with an axe or a sword,' replied the princess. 'The life of the giant is in an egg and it is the egg you must crush to kill the giant.'

'And where shall I find the egg?' he asked.

'It is kept by an old witch who lives in the woods nearby and you must destroy her before you can find the egg. Once found it will easily be broken and once broken we are all safe,' replied the princess. She told him how to find the witch's house and then immediately fell back asleep.

So the young lad set off again and soon reached the house of the witch. He saw her sitting shivering and huddled in front of the fire. He opened the door and went inside.

'Good morning,' he said. 'I see you are not well, old wife. Is there anything I can do for you?'

'Yes,' she said, 'if you would carry me outside into the fresh air I would feel better.'

The young lad took her up on his back but quick as a blink he tossed her on to the fire. Up the chimney she went with a noise like rumbling thunder. The poor widow's son lost no time and began to look for the egg. He searched and he searched and eventually he found it in a dark, dusty cupboard. He put in on to the floor and crushed it beneath his boot. Splat!

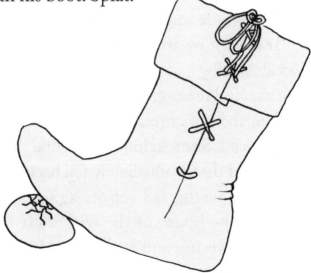

At that very moment, outside the castle, the giant let out an enormous roar and fell down dead with a tremendous crash right where he stood. People across that land heard the noise and wondered what had happened.

Inside the castle, all those who'd been kept asleep as prisoners began to wake up and one by one they learned the story of the poor widow's son from the king's daughter. By the time he arrived back he was a hero.

The young lad returned the princess to her father, King Malcolm, who gave him her hand in marriage.

So the poor widow was poor no longer and the young couple lived a long and happy life. It is thought the Dukes of Buccleuch are descended from this marriage.

And the stranger remained just that, a mysterious stranger.

Mind the Crooked Finger

SHETLAND

Once a farmer and his wife lived at Kirgood-a-Weisdale in Shetland and they had just had a pretty baby and in the days that followed they had many visitors. So it was on this particular afternoon that the wise woman and some others had come to see the new baby and keep the young mother company.

The farmer set about his afternoon chores but just as he was leaving the lamb-house at twilight he heard three most unearthly knocks. It seemed as if they came from under the ground. He didn't know what this could be, and although he was very frightened, he went up to the corn yard and as he came in sight of the barn he heard voices, muttering and arguing. He wondered what was going on when a voice said loudly, 'Mind the crooked finger!'

Remember the crooked finger? The farmer listened closely, since his wife had a crooked finger. Twice more he heard the voice, 'Mind the crooked finger!'

The young farmer trembled all the more for he knew that something bad was going to happen. He knew that trolls were often on the lookout for any helpless baby, or new mother, or both. He had to protect his family. If there were trolls in the barn he knew just what to do.

He ran back into the house, lit a candle, and picked up the Bible and a knife.

Suddenly, as he opened the book, there came a roaring and unearthly stamping and rattling from the barn. It was so loud that it made the whole house shake and everybody quaked with fear.

The farmer asked the wise woman to stay with his wife and baby and he left for the barn. The rest of the visitors followed him, eyes wide with fear. He had the Bible in one hand, held the knife between his teeth, and the burning candle in his other hand. When he got to the barn door the noise was deafening but – throwing the Bible in before him – he stepped inside.

Instantly all was silence.

The others crowded in behind him and there they saw the strangest thing. It was an image, a model, an exact copy of his wife right down to her crooked finger!

The trolls had gone.

'Well,' said the farmer, 'the trolls meant to put you into my house and steal away my real wife, but I will make use of you in a different way.'

He carried the trolls' model into the house and they all saw it was indeed a very fine copy of his wife. He sat it on a stool and there it stayed for many a year. Why, little children used to climb up and sit happily in its lap!

And that's as true as I'm writing this for you, and not a borrowed or handed-down story; for Bill Robertson of Lerwick said his mother told the story with her own lips, and she would not have told him a lie for she was there, in that house, that very night.

Habetrot

BORDERS

In the beautiful countryside of Selkirkshire, there lived a guidwife who had a pretty daughter, who loved to be outside in the fields and the woods all day. That was all well and good when she was young but as the girl grew older her mother tried to teach her to bake and to spin, for these were the skills she would need if she were to marry well.

The girl did not mind baking but she did not like spinning. She didn't have the patience to sit and concentrate and she would leave her spinning, run out of the cottage and across the fields as free as the larks in the sky. Her mother could do nothing to make the girl understand that she must learn to spin.

Finally, one spring morning, the guidwife brought out seven bundles of flax and told the girl she must have them spun into yarn in three days.

'If you cannot do this then you will be good for nothing but work in the pigsty!'

The girl knew her mother meant what she said and so she sat and began to work, teasing out the fine threads, licking her fingers to make sure she had a smooth yarn. She worked all day until her fingers and her shoulders ached but at the end of the day she had only spun a very short length of yarn. She cried herself to sleep but on the second day she was up as early as the birds to begin work. Her mother encouraged her but by the end of the day the poor girl was in tears again. Her lips were sore and her fingers red and still she had only spun quite a short length of yarn.

Early in the morning on the third day the young girl took one look at those seven bundles of flax and pushed them aside. She ran out of the house, through the fields sparkling with dew and down to the little burn in the woods.

Here there were pretty flowers, birds singing and the water in the burn babbled over the stones. She sat down and hid her face in her hands. She did not know what to do.

When she finally looked up she was surprised to see an old lady on the other side of the burn, sitting in the sunshine on a self-bored stone. Such stones had holes bored through them by the running waters of rivers and were said to be doorways into the land of the wee folk. The girl looked more closely. The old lady was licking her fingers and drawing out flax and the girl noticed the lady's lips were swollen and red.

'Good morning Grannie,' she called out as she got up. Being curious she added, 'What has happed to your lips?'

'Ah,' said the old dame, pleased to meet such a friendly girl, 'that comes from spinning thread, my hinnie.'

The girl sighed, 'I should be spinning too, but try as I might I cannot finish the task my mother set for me.'

The old lady asked about the task and the young girl told her, ending in tears, 'I have tried and tried and I want to please my mother but I cannot do it!'

The little lady offered to spin the thread for her so the girl ran as fast as her legs would carry her to collect the bundles of flax. Back she raced through the fields and down to the burn. She paddled through the water and gave the flax to the old woman.

'What is your name and when should I return to collect the spinning?' the girl asked as she crossed back across the burn. There was no reply. The lady had vanished. The poor girl wandered up and down wondering what to do until worn out, she fell asleep against a tree.

When she woke, Causleen, the evening star, was shining and the moon was rising.

All was still and quiet but then she heard a voice coming across the burn. She waded over and sure enough she clearly heard a voice that seemed to come from the self-bored stone. She put her ear over the hole and she heard, 'Little kens the lassie, my name is Habetrot.'

Habetrot! The girl could not believe her ears so she peered through the hole. There in a deep cavern below she saw the kindly old lady walking up and down between a group of spinsters all busy with distaffs and spindles. In the Borderlands, Habetrot was known to be the fairy guardian of spinning wheels and friend of all spinners. The old lady encouraged the spinners and they seemed to be happy at their work but oh dear … every one of them had long, drooping, swollen lips just like Habetrot's. One of them had bulging grey eyes and a great hooked nose and she was reeling the yarn.

Habetot called to this odd lady, 'Scantlie Mab have you nearly finished measuring and reeling up the yarn for the lassie? She must go home to her mother soon.'

The girl slipped away back across the burn to wait and think about what she had seen. Shortly afterwards there was the old woman crossing the burn with the hanks of spun yarn.

'Oh thank you,' said the happy girl, 'and what can I do for you in return?'

'Nothing, nothing,' replied the old lady, 'but do not tell your mother who spun the yarn.'

The girl set off through the dark hardly able to believe her good fortune. When she got home she found her mother had already gone to bed. She laid out the seven hanks of yarn and realised she was hungry. There, hanging in the chimney to dry were seven puddings. Her mother had been busy all day she could see. The girl took one down and fried it over the fire and ate it up in no time at all. In fact she was so hungry she ate them one by one, all seven! Then she went to bed.

In the morning the guidwife was up early as usual and came into the kitchen to find her puddings all gone. On the table she saw the seven hanks of smooth yarn. She was so surprised she went outside saying over and over again in delight:

My daughter's spun seven, seven, seven!
My daughter's eaten seven, seven, seven!
And all before daylight!

Suddenly she heard hoof beats and looking up she saw the young laird riding by and she bobbed a curtsy. He asked what was the matter and so she said it again:

My daughter's spun seven, seven, seven!
My daughter's eaten seven, seven, seven!
And if you don't believe me,
Come in and see!

The curious laird followed the woman into the cottage and there on the table he saw the seven hanks of finely spun yarn. He'd never seen such fine yarn and certainly none of the skilled, fine ladies he knew could spin like this! So he asked to meet the spinner. The proud woman fetched her daughter and the girl stood by the table blushing. She blushed because there stood the young laird and on the table was the yarn she had not spun.

The laird immediately fell in love with her and explained how he had long been searching for a bride. She was both bonny and the finest spinner he had ever met and he asked her to be his wife.

So they were engaged to be married but now the girl began to worry. She knew that of all the tasks she would have to perform as wife of the laird, spinning would be the most important. All women could spin for how else were clothes and sheets to be made? She would have other maidens in the castle to help of course but she would have to sit with them and encourage them just as Habetrot encouraged her spinsters. No more walks across the sunlit fields. No more visits to the little flower-filled glen by the burn. Then she had an idea.

She set off across the fields and down to the little burn in the woods. She crossed to the self-bored stone and called down the hole, 'Habetrot? Habetrot?'

Suddenly old Habetrot was there beside her and the girl told her what had happened. While she was pleased by her good fortune she was also worried.

'I cannot spin!' she wept, 'I want to be a good wife, but I cannot spin.'

The old woman spoke kindly, 'Once you are married bring your bonny bridegroom here. Once he sees what comes of spinning he'll never ask you to spin at all!'

So after the wedding the girl led her new husband across the fields and down to the burn. They crossed the burn together and she whispered through the hole in the self-bored stone, 'Habetrot? Habetrot, I have brought my husband.' The girl told him to look through the hole and to his great surprise he saw the spinsters sat upon their stones, hard at work with distaffs and spindles. He watched as they licked their fingers over their drooping, swollen lips to draw out the threads.

Suddenly one of them looked up.

'Who's that peeping through the stone?' asked Scantlie Mab.

'A guest I have invited,' replied Habetrot, who opened a secret door at the root of the tree. 'Come in, come in!' she called to the girl and her husband.

The young laird had never seen such weird women; every one of them had long, drooping, swollen lips. He asked each of them what had happened to cause such a deformity. In reply one after the other they spluttered words he could not make out. He shook his head saying he did not understand what they were saying so they each took up their flax and licked their fingers and showed him!

Habetrot stood beside the young girl, gave her a wink and called the laird to her side. She gave the girl her distaff and spindle and told her to spin. The lass licked her fingers, pouted her pretty lips and began to spin but the laird grabbed the flax from her hands.

'You will never touch a distaff or wheel again my dear love,' he vowed.

She never did. All the flax grown on their land she took to Habetrot to be spun into thread. And so it was that the young girl kept her bonny looks, the laird was pleased and Habetrot and her spinsters were kept busy.

The Puddock

FIFE

Once there was a poor widow who lived with her daughter. One day she decided to bake some bannocks, little flat cakes, for their supper. She got everything ready and told her daughter to take a dish and go to the well for some water.

The lassie took the dish and she walked to the well but she found it was dry. There was no water! The poor lass couldn't go home without water and she didn't know what to do so she sat beside the well and began to cry.

Then a wee puddock, a little frog, came a leap, leap, leaping from out of the well and sat down beside her.

'Why are you crying?' he asked her.

Now, the lassie didn't like frogs so she turned away but she said, 'I'm crying because there is no water in the well and my mother needs water to bake some bannocks.'

'Then stop crying,' said the puddock, 'for if you promise to marry me you will have all the water you need.'

The lassie couldn't believe the frog was serious. He must be joking! She began to cry again and the wee frog said, 'All you have to do is promise to marry me.'

'Very well then,' she said, 'I promise to marry you.'

She heard water bubbling in the well, filled her dish and hurried off home as fast as she could. She thought no more about the frog until later that night just as she and her mother were about to go to their beds. There was a knocking on the door and they heard singing:

Oh open the door, my hinnie, my heart,
Oh open the door, my own true love,
Remember the promise you made to me,
Down in the meadow, where we two met.

'Go and see who's at the door,' said the mother to her daughter.

So the lassie opened the door and looked out.
Then she looked down and saw the frog on the
doorstep.

She shut the door quickly.

'Who is out there?' asked the woman.

'Hoot,' said the daughter, 'it's nothing but a
filthy yellow puddock.'

'Open the door and let the poor puddock
come in,' said her mother.

So the lassie opened the door and the
puddock came a leap, leap, leaping in and sat
down by the fireside.

He began to sing:

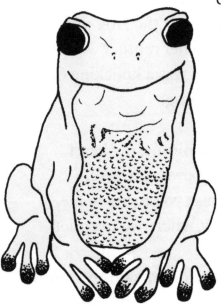

Oh give me my supper, my hinnie, my heart,
Oh give me my supper, my own true love,
Remember the promise you made to me,
Down in the meadow, where we two met.

'Hoot,' scoffed the daughter, 'would I be giving
a wee puddock his supper? I don't think so!'

'Oh aye,' said her mother, 'give the poor
puddock his supper.'

So the puddock got his supper and after that
he began to sing:

Oh put me to bed, my hinnie, my heart,
Oh put me to bed, my own true love,
Remember the promise you made to me,
Down in the meadow, where we two met.

'Hoot,' sneered the daughter, 'would I be putting
a filthy puddock to bed? I don't think so!'

'Oh aye,' said her mother, 'put the poor
puddock to bed.'

The girl bent down and picked up the wee
frog and with her arms fully outstretched away
from her she carried him and dropped him on

the floor by the bed. She wiped her hands on her apron.

Then the puddock sang again:

Now fetch me an axe, my hinnie, my heart,
Now fetch me an axe, my own true love,
Remember the promise you made to me
Down in the meadow, where we two met.

Well she didn't like frogs did she, so the lassie was not long in fetching the axe and then the puddock sang:

Now chop off my head, my hinnie, my heart,
Now chop off my head, my own true love
Remember the promise you made to me,
Down in the meadow, where we two met.

The lassie looked at the puddock and she thought she couldn't do such a thing for he was such a feisty wee creature who'd done her no harm.

'Hoot,' she said, 'would I be chopping the head off a poor wee puddock? I don't think so!'

'Oh aye,' said her mother, 'do as the poor puddock says.'

So she shut her eyes, lifted the axe and brought it down with a crash. When she opened her eyes to look for the poor puddock she saw a pair of feet. On top of the feet was a pair of long, strong legs. On top of those legs was the rest of the bonniest young prince that ever was seen. And he sang:

> Oh marry me now, my hinnie, my heart,
> You have broken the spell, my own true love,
> Remember the promise you made to me,
> Down in the meadow, where we two met.

'Hoot,' said the lassie, 'would I be marrying a bonny young prince?'

'Oh, aye,' said her mother, 'you must keep your promise.'

So she did!

Assipattle and the Giant Mester Stoor Worm

ORKNEY

Long, long ago when the world was still new, there lived a gigantic sea serpent so big that his body coiled right around the world twice, below the oceans. When he was hungry he opened his great jaws, sucked in the sea, everything in the sea and everything on the sea, deep, deep down into the twists and turns of his long body. The seawater ran down the beaches leaving great stretches of sand. When he was satisfied, hours later, he spewed out any rubbish and the seawater he did not need and this rushed back up the beaches. Anyone standing on a beach and seeing that would know that the Mester Stoor Worm was nearby. Sometimes he was not satisfied with food from the sea so he used his great forked tongue to reach out across the land sweeping whole herds of sheep and cattle into his mouth.

Now one day the Mester Stoor Worm came to the lands in the far north. His enormous head rose above the sea like a huge island. It could be seen for miles and miles. The king was worried. The people were terrified. Only one person was not afraid and that was Assipattle.

Assipattle was the youngest of seven sons. He lived with his father, mother and brothers on a fine farm and while there was always plenty of work to be done Assipattle did very little of it. He preferred to lie beside the big fire in the kitchen and so he was always covered in ashes, which is how he got his name, which means paddling in the ashes.

His mother and father shook their heads over him and his brothers teased him and called him a fool, but they all laughed and laughed when Assipattle told stories late at night. These were stories of great battles and Assipattle was always the hero.

When news of the giant Mester Stoor Worm reached the farm, Assipattle's mother cried out, 'What will become of us? The Mester Stoor Worm has to be fed or he will destroy the land. What will the king do?'

'Never mind the king,' said Assipattle, 'I'm going to kill the Mester Stoor Worm.'

'You!' teased his brothers, 'you are good for nothing but lying by the fire and telling stories.'

'You wait and see,' said Assipattle. 'I'll fight the Stoor Worm and live to tell the story to my children's children.'

Just as everyone expected, the hungry Stoor Worm searched the land with his great forked tongue sweeping aside any buildings in his path. He licked up chickens and children and he munched and crunched whole flocks of sheep. The people were desperate. They went to the king and begged him to stop the Stoor Worm.

The king summoned a spaeman, a wise man, and asked him to find a way to save the land and his people. The wise man thought and thought.

'The only way to keep the Stoor Worm happy,' he told the king, 'is to feed him seven maidens every week.'

The people were horrified but the danger was so great that there seemed to be no choice. The sad king agreed.

So on Saturday seven maidens were bound hand and foot and taken to the rocks by the edge of the sea. The Stoor Worm raised his head, reached out with his forked tongue and in an instant all seven were gone. The people could not believe this was the only solution so they went to the king and pleaded, 'Surely there is some other way to stop the Stoor Worm.'

Once again the king asked the spaeman who thought and thought and by the time he had the answer he was trembling with fear, 'The Stoor Worm will only be satisfied once he has the most beautiful girl in the land,' he said, 'your own daughter, Princess Gem-de-Lovely.'

The king loved his only daughter above all else but he saw the grief and suffering of his people and with tears rolling down his cheeks he agreed.

His brave daughter spoke up, 'I am a princess descended from Viking blood,' said Gem-de-Lovely, 'and I shall do this for my people. May the great God Odin help me!'

'You are a brave young lady,' said the spaeman. 'Maybe your bravery will be matched by some young warrior who will come to fight the Stoor Worm and your life will be spared.'

The king knew there was only one chance to save his lovely daughter and he announced, 'We must rid the land of the giant Mester Stoor Worm. I shall send messengers far and wide to proclaim that any man who is brave enough and strong enough to overcome this monster shall have the hand of Gem-de-Lovely in marriage.'

And so messengers rode out far and wide across the lands of the far north. When the king's messenger arrived at Assipattle's farm the family gathered to hear the news.

'I shall fight the Stoor Worm,' said Assipattle immediately, 'I've been saving my strength all these years for just such a fight.'

Assipattle's brothers laughed and shoved him out of the way and his father shook his head and said crossly, 'Be off with you lazy boy!'

But Assipattle stayed right where he was and listened.

The messenger continued, 'Thirty-six champions came but twenty-four of those turned and ran at the very sight of the Mester Stoor Worm. The other twelve are sick with fear and the king has no faith in them. As old and feeble as he is, the king has taken down the great sword Sikkersnapper, the sword of Odin, and he will fight the Stoor Worm himself. His boat is ready and huge crowds are gathering to see the battle tomorrow.'

Assipattle listened carefully. The only way to reach the king's Long House so far away would be to take Teitgong, his father's magic horse. Teitgong could fly faster than the wind. However, the horse would let no one but the farmer ride him.

'I'd like to see that battle,' said Assipattle's mother that evening.

'We'd have to take Teitgong, for no other horse could cover that distance in time,' replied his father, 'but I have no wish to see our king eaten by a monster.'

Now his wife dearly wanted to discover the secrets about Teitgong. For years she had tried to find out why no one but her husband could ride the horse and so that night she nagged and nagged her husband.

Assipattle lay beside the fire with his eyes shut and his ears open and at last his father gave in with a sigh, 'When I want Teitgong to stand I pat his left shoulder and when I want him to trot off I give him two pats on the right shoulder. But when I want him to gallop as fast as he can, I blow through the goose thrapple that I keep safely in the pocket of my jacket,' he told her. 'When Teitgong hears that whistle he flies like the wind.'

Assipattle lay still and silent until he knew his parents were asleep. Then up he got and stole the goose thrapple from his father's jacket pocket and crept to the stable. When he first tried to catch Teitgong, the horse reared and kicked but Assipattle only had to pat his left shoulder and the horse became quiet as a mouse. Then Assipattle mounted Teitgong, patted his right shoulder twice and they were off with a loud neigh and a great clattering of hooves. The noise woke the farmer.

'Quick! Everyone get up! Saddle the best horses. Teitgong has been stolen,' he shouted, waking up the entire household.

Soon they were off after the stolen horse. It wasn't long before the farmer was hard on the heels of Teitgong and he called out, 'Hi, hi, ho! Teitgong whoa.'

Teitgong drew up to a halt but Assipattle pulled out the goose thrapple and blew as hard as he could. Immediately Teitgong galloped off faster than the wind. He galloped so fast that Assipattle could hardly breathe, leaving his father and brothers far behind.

They reached the coast just before dawn and came to a halt by a cottage in the sand dunes, high above the beach. Down below, in the shallow waters, Assipattle saw the king's boat. Sitting inside the boat was a guard and far out

to sea was a great mountain, the head of the Mester Stoor Worm.

Assipattle left Teitgong and slipped inside the wee cottage. An old woman slept soundly on her bed and Assipattle crept to the fire she had banked up for the night. He took an empty iron cooking pot and into this he placed a lump of glowing peat from the fire. Carrying the iron pot, he crept back out of the house as quietly as he could, while the grey cat sleeping on the end of the old woman's bed stretched and yawned.

Assipattle made his way down to the shore and greeted the guard who was sitting shivering in the boat. 'It's a cold morning,' said Assipattle as he set down the pot and started gathering some driftwood for a fire. 'Why don't you come and warm yourself?'

'I would if I could,' replied the man, 'but I cannot leave the king's boat unguarded.'

'You'd better stay where you are then,' said Assipattle. 'I'll just light a fire and cook some limpets for my breakfast.' He began to dig a hollow in the sand as if to set the fire and then he jumped up shouting, 'Gold! It must be buried treasure!'

Assipattle started digging again, pretending to fill his pockets with golden coins. All the while he watched until, from the corner of his eye, he saw the guard leap out of the boat and come wading ashore. He knocked Assipattle out of the way and began digging furiously.

This was Assipattle's chance! He grabbed the pot with the glowing peat inside and ran to the boat. He was well out to sea by the time the guard realised he'd been tricked. The guard roared so loudly that the king and his men came running down to the beach and

they watched as Assipattle hoisted the sail and
steered the boat towards the monster. The head
of the giant Mester Stoor Worm rested on the
sea like a huge mountain and Assipattle knew
he had to be in just the right place before the
Stoor Worm woke up and yawned.

He waited for the sun to rise and, at last, the
Stoor Worm blinked and slowly he opened
his great jaws and flicked his forked tongue.
Assipattle steadied the boat and pointed it
right at the gaping mouth.

Then he felt the sea swell as the monster
began to suck into his great mouth everything
in the sea and on the sea including Assipattle
and the boat.

Before he knew it Assipattle was swept on
and on down the Stoor Worm's throat and
beyond, into the long tunnel of his body.

For mile after mile, he crouched in the boat as it was swirled deeper and deeper into the Stoor Worm. Then, as the tunnel became narrower and the flood of seawater became shallower, the boat suddenly stopped. The mast was jammed on the Stoor Worm's ribs and the boat was grounded.

Assipattle jumped out carrying the iron pot and ran as fast as he could even deeper into the Stoor Worm. A glimmering light from the peat lit up the dark tunnel and before too long he'd found the creature's liver. He wasted no time, took out his knife and cut a deep hole into the

liver. Into the hole he tipped the glowing peat and then he blew. He blew and he blew until the peat burned and a small flame appeared. He blew and he blew until the fire took hold and then Assipattle grabbed the cooking pot, turned and ran. He had to return the pot to the old woman. He ran faster than he'd ever run in his life and clambered back into the boat just in time.

On the shore the king and his men watched and a crowd gathered.

'Look,' shouted the king, 'there's smoke! The Stoor Worm is on fire!'

The Stoor Worm started to feel mighty sick and he retched and he retched and he spewed out all that he had sucked in – the seawater, everything in the sea and on the sea including Assipattle in the boat. The flood of water was so great that the boat carrying Assipattle shot straight up the beach and landed high and dry at the foot of the sand dunes. Everyone ran from the rushing seawater and stood on the sand dunes high up by the cottage where the old woman and her grey cat had been woken by the roaring of the Mester Stoor Worm. They all watched, the king and his men, the guard, the old woman and at the back of the crowd, Assipattle's father and his brothers.

'Arrest that man,' called the guard.

'No!' cried Gem-de-Lovely. 'Look!' She ran to Assipattle and took his hand.

Billowing black clouds of smoke swirled from the monster's nostrils.

The giant Mester Stoor Worm lifted his head and shot out his forked tongue until it reached up into the sky where it took a slice out of the moon. As the great forked tongue slammed back into the earth it made an enormous rift

that divided the lands of Sweden and Finland. The rift filled with seawater and became known as the Baltic Sea.

The Stoor Worm rose up again, twisting and turning and dashing his head back down to the earth so hard that the whole world shook and groaned. Teeth fell from its jaws and these became the Orkney Islands. Again the beast reared and again he fell back and the teeth that fell this time became the Shetland Islands. For a third and last time the Stoor Worm raised his head, groaned and smashed it back down and the teeth that fell became the Faroe Islands. Finally the Stoor Worm sank below the sea.

When the world was quiet again and the smoke had cleared from the sky the king took Assipattle into his arms and called him his son. He gave him his own cloak and the hand of Gem-de-Lovely and about his waist he girded the great sword of Odin, Sikkersnapper.

'As far as my kingdom stretches, north, south, east and west, everything belongs to this hero who has saved our land and our people,' he proclaimed.

And so Assipattle and Gem-de-Lovely were married. Never was there such a wedding in the lands of the north for everyone in the kingdom was happy. There was singing and dancing all over the country and King Assipattle and Queen Gem-de-Lovely were happy too for they were both brave and loved each other.

They had ever so many fine children and their children had children and so on down through the years until one of those great, great, great, great, great, great, great, great, great, great, great, great ... grandchildren told me the story I have just told you.

BUT,

If you are ever standing on a beach and watching the seawater rushing down and then, hours later, see it rushing back up the beach you will know that the giant Mester Stoor Worm is not dead. The old folk say that he sleeps beneath a country in the cold North Sea and there, beneath the snow-covered mountains, the Stoor Worm's liver still burns, which is why, even in the coldest winters there are hot springs in Iceland.

The Shepherd of Kintail

HIGHLANDS

Once there was a shepherd who lived in Kintail. It is a wild and rugged region in the West Highlands and to make a living there was very difficult. So every summer the shepherd would take his sheep away up the glen where there was plenty of sweet grass for them to eat.

There he lived in a bothy, a little stone hut, all by himself with just his dog to keep him company. His bed was made with heather and he had a chair beside the fire where he cooked his simple meals. He wore a plaid, a great length of tartan woven wool that he could gather around his waist into a kilt, held there by a leather belt. If it was chilly he could use one end of the cloth to make a cloak over his white linen shirt. At night he could use it as a blanket. He had everything he needed for this simple life.

One evening towards the end of summer the weather became quite cool. The shepherd knew the sheep were safe with his dog and so he lit a fire and lay down on his bed for a few hours' sleep.

Sometime later he awoke to the strangest sight. There, sat by his fire, was a row of cats warming their paws. Each one had a black cap.

One of the cats got up and went to the little window, put on its cap and said, 'Hurrah for London!' It disappeared! One by one the other cats went to the little window and did the same thing, but the cap of the last cat fell off just as the cat vanished. The curious shepherd left his bed, picked up the cap and went to the little window. He put on the cap and said, 'Hurrah for London!'

And suddenly there he was in London following the cats down into a cellar where they began to drink wine. So the shepherd drank wine with the cats but he had too much, got drunk and fell asleep. The astonished owner of the cellar found him in the morning.

'Who are you? What are you doing here?' he asked the strange-looking person. No one in London dressed in this odd fashion!

Well the poor shepherd was speaking Gaelic of course and he tried to explain but the cellar man could not understand a word so he called the police. They arrested the shepherd and took him to a judge who realised the shepherd was a Highlander. He sent for a man who could understand the language.

'Now tell us how you came to be in a locked cellar and how will you pay the owner for the wine you have drunk?' asked the judge. 'It was a mighty lot of wine!' he commented.

Again the shepherd tried to explain what had happened and when he said the cats had been drinking wine everyone in the court laughed. Of course no one believed him so the judge shook his head, 'Not only are you a thief but I think you are also quite mad. Since you cannot pay the cellar man you will have to go to gaol.'

The police took the poor shepherd to the gaol and the gaoler locked him in a dark, damp cell. He looked around and then before the gaoler and the policeman left he called out, 'I would like my black cap please,' he said and, hoping they would feel sorry for him, he added, 'my mother gave it to me.'

He looked so sad that the policeman went to fetch the cap and poked it through the bars. The shepherd quickly went to the little barred window, put the cap on his head and shouted, 'Hurrah for Kintail!'

And just as suddenly as before there he was, back in his bothy in Kintail. He opened the door and there stood some of his very surprised friends, since his dog had raised the alarm after his master went missing. They asked him what had happened but this time the shepherd decided he would not try to explain. For no one would believe him, would they?

Thomas the Rhymer

BORDERS

In the Borders of Scotland, a long time ago, there lived a young man called Thomas Learmont of Ercildoune. He lived in a strong Tower House and was Laird of all the beautiful lands close by. All those years ago few people could read or write but Thomas liked to make rhymes, to sing and play the harp.

One day, while Thomas was walking in the woods he heard the tinkling of little bells. Through the trees he saw a beautiful lady riding a dapple-grey horse. She was dressed in the greens of the forest and her long hair was the colour of ripened corn. She wore a crown of gold sparkling with emeralds and rubies. There were more jewels on her fingers and her horse had silver reins and an ivory-white saddle. The jingling bells were threaded in its long flowing mane. Thomas took off his hat and bowed very low.

'Welcome to my lands, fair lady,' said Thomas. 'Who are you?'

'I am the queen of a faraway land,' laughed the beautiful lady. 'I have come for you Thomas, to hear your rhymes and to hear you play your harp.'

Thomas could not help falling under her spell.

They sat under the Eildon Tree and he sang the old ballads of the Borders and played his harp until at last the lady asked, 'Have you a kiss for the Queen of Elfland?'

Thomas did not think twice and gave her the kiss she wanted but she laughed gently, 'Your kiss has cost you seven years, Thomas. For seven years you shall be my servant.'

Thomas shook his head. He had been tricked. 'Please forgive me,' he begged. 'I have my family and my lands to look after.'

But the lady said, 'Come Thomas, ride with me to Elfland. You cannot refuse this queen and I have chosen you because we fairies love the music of the Borders. You shall play for us.'

Thomas was very frightened but he climbed onto the back of the strong horse. For a long time Thomas rode behind the Queen of Elfland but eventually they came to a halt on the edge of a bleak moor and the queen spoke softly.

'There are only three roads in life Thomas, but few mortals see them. Look carefully now,' she said.

As the moorland melted before his eyes sure enough he could see three roads and the queen pointed to a broad, level road.

'That is an easy road, often taken by lazy people, and if you chose that road through life you might come to a bad end.' Next she pointed towards a hidden, twisted and steep pathway through briars and brambles. 'Very few men take that path. It needs a strong heart and hard work to travel that long and weary way. It leads to peace and happiness.'

'And the third road?' Thomas asked. He looked at the gentle pathway leading between the bracken and the yellow of the broom.

The queen sighed happily, 'That, my dear Thomas, is a road few mortals can walk for it leads to Elfland. That is our road, the road to my homeland.'

Thomas looked behind him sadly but his home was far, far away.

'Thomas,' said the queen kindly, 'listen carefully if you want to see your home and family again. For seven years you will serve me in Elfland and for seven years you must not speak.

Remember, one word from your lips will make you my servant forever.'

Thomas shut his lips tight as they set off down the road to Elfland.

It was a long journey and the road became narrower and narrower as they went deeper and deeper into a ravine. Soon it was so dark Thomas could not see. He could smell the damp and woody earth, and he could hear the running of water in little burns. He felt the branches of the trees catching at his clothes as they passed.

At last, after many hours, the sun appeared. All around were beautiful fruit trees and Thomas smelt the warm, ripe pears, apples and cherries. The grass was wet with dew and he saw bright red strawberries. He longed for something to eat.

The queen spoke to him, 'While you are in Elfland, Thomas, you must eat nothing except the apple I will give to you. If you eat anything else you will be poisoned and you will remain in Elfland forever.'

She reached into the branches of a small tree bursting with glossy red apples and picked just one. 'These are the Apples of Truth. Once you have eaten this, Thomas, no lie will pass from your lips.'

The queen pointed to a hillside where a dazzling castle gleamed in the sunlight. Its tall towers reached up into the blue sky. 'There is my home,' she said. She pulled out her hunting horn and blew so loud and strong that Thomas wondered how anyone could have so much breath! He got off the horse and was about to speak but he remembered what she had said and put his hand over his mouth instead.

She smiled at him, 'You do well to remember Thomas, and now you are my pageboy. Here come the folk of Elfland to welcome us.'

The wee folk skipped and hopped and cheered as Thomas led the queen along the road up to the castle.

They all trooped into the main hall where the king sat on his tall throne. Before she sat down on her own throne, the queen gave Thomas a harp.

'I will call you to play for my Lord the King,' she said. 'We love the music from your world.'

Thomas found himself a seat where he was out of the way and as he tuned the harp he watched. There was a great deal of noise and people were running to and fro. Servants set up long tables for a great feast. Cooks brought in roasted meats and enormous pies. Kitchen maids carried jugs of wine and towering baskets of fruits. All the time Thomas watched and kept his lips firmly closed. He took none of the fine food and nothing to drink.

The feasting went on through the night. There was singing and dancing and Thomas clapped his hands and tapped his feet. It seemed as if no one wanted to sleep. Thomas smiled at them but he remembered to eat no food and to say not one word.

At last the queen called to Thomas. He passed through the crowd with his harp and sat at the feet of the queen. He played the soft haunting songs of his homeland. The great hall grew quiet.

Thomas played until the first rays of the sun crept over the edge of the earth. Now almost everyone had fallen asleep.

'Come Thomas!' said the queen, 'You have done well and now you can return to your Tower House.'

Thomas was amazed and almost spoke but he remembered the warning just in time and shut his lips tight. 'This must be a trick!' he thought. 'I have not been here for seven years.'

'You do well to remember your silence Thomas,' laughed the queen, 'but truly you have been here for seven years. However, if you would like to stay forever you only need to ask me.'

Thomas looked round the lovely hall and then at the beautiful queen and he shook his head. No matter how wonderful it was he could not stay. It was time to return to his homeland.

Once again Thomas rode on the dapple-grey horse behind the queen. They travelled the long journey until at last he was home on the edge of the woods.

When Thomas slipped down from the horse he cleared his throat. It was strange to hear his voice after such a long silence.

'Thank you for the gift of truth My Lady, but may I have a small token to remember my visit to Elfland.'

'I shall give you the gift of prophesy so you may foretell the future. You shall be known as True Thomas for your truth and as Thomas the Rhymer for your poems. For your prophecies you will be remembered for all time,' she replied.

'Thank you,' he said, 'but will I ever see you again?'

She smiled and from her saddlebag she took a beautifully carved harp. It was decorated with gold and inset with mother of pearl and brightly coloured enamels.

'Think of me when you play, Thomas. One day I shall send for you.'

When Thomas walked into his own great hall his poor family had such a shock, 'Thomas! We have waited for seven long years! Where have you been?'

Thomas shook his head. He could not say he had been to Elfland but he could not tell a lie, 'I have been travelling far away and I have learned many things,' he said.

As time passed people forgot how Thomas had disappeared for seven years. They often admired the beautiful harp but Thomas never told them it had come from Elfland.

One night Thomas dreamt about a terrible storm. He saw the king riding through the wind and rain and he saw an accident. Thomas knew this was the queen's gift of prophecy.

On the very next day, March 19th in 1286, King Alexander III rode from Edinburgh and crossed the Firth of Forth in a boat at Queensferry. The king rode through a storm but his horse stumbled and he fell to his death over the cliffs at Kinghorn in Fife.

People remembered that Thomas had foretold the king's death. He became known as a wise man and folk came to him for advice when they had problems. Thomas always told them the truth.

The rhymes and prophesies of Thomas were often curious because they told about things that would happen in the future. Thomas was a very old man by this time, and though he never spoke of it, he had never forgotten his visit to the magical world of Elfland.

One moonlit night, the guards on the tower saw a strange sight. Two white deer, a hart and a hind were making their way through the trees in the parklands. They stood and waited close by the great gates.

'I've never seen white deer before,' muttered one of the men.

'It must be an omen,' said the other. 'We must tell Thomas.'

Old Thomas smiled when he heard the news. 'At last the messengers have come from Elfland. I must go.'

He picked up his harp and went into the moonlit garden.

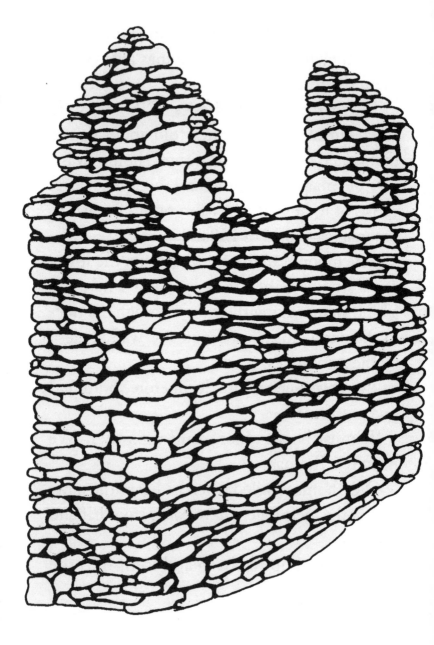

The snow-white deer waited for him and led Thomas into the woods, through the trees and across the river. They were never seen again.

Thomas had returned to Elfland.

The ruins of Thomas's old Tower House still stand between the river called Leader Water and the town, now known as Earlston. The Queen of Elfland was right of course because all these hundreds of years later we still remember Thomas the Rhymer.

Why the Sea is Salty

ORKNEY

Long, long ago seawater was just the same as rainwater and the water in rivers and in lakes.

At that time the King of Denmark was King Frodi and he owned an enormous quern, two huge round stones set one upon the other to make an enormous hand mill. The name of this mill was Grotti. The quern had been given to him by a giant and it was magic for it would grind out whatever it was commanded to. However, King Frodi could not use the quern because he could find no one strong enough to turn the stones.

One day he set sail to visit the King of Sweden, King Fjolnir.

'Have you come to seek a wife?' asked King Fjolnir.

'Oh no,' replied King Frodi, 'but I have come to find a pair of your strongest working girls, for though the girls in Denmark may be pretty, they are weak.'

King Fjolnir called for Fenia and Menia, both daughters of a giant, and so King Frodi returned to Denmark with the girls and set them to working the mill.

'Grind me some gold,' he ordered the girls and so they set to and ground out gold, day after day, night after night.

'When may we rest?' the girls asked the king.

'When the cuckoo stops singing,' said the king. 'Now grind me some peace for the land.'

So they set to and ground out peace, day after day, night after night.

'When may we rest?' the girls asked the king.

'When the cuckoo stops singing,' said the king. 'Now grind me some happiness for my people.'

So they set to and ground out happiness, day after day, night after night.

'We cannot rest for the cuckoo never stops singing,' the girls said to the king. 'We are tired. When may we sleep?'

'You may sleep only when you are singing,' replied the greedy king.

The girls were very angry for they could *not* sleep and sing at the same time and so as they turned the great millstones they began to sing a strange song. They sang for an army with a million horses; they sang for myriads of men; they sang for a fleet of pirates to come and kill the king who had made them slaves.

In the dead of night Mysingr, a sea-king, came with a fleet of pirate ships and thousands of men. They killed King Frodi and peace was ended. They stole the gold, the magic quern and the two giant girls, Fenia and Menia.

Mysingr set sail again heading for Scotland and immediately ordered the girls to grind out salt.

'Salt is more precious than gold,' he said, 'and I shall sell it to the kings of the world.'

So they set to and ground out salt all day and into the night.

'May we rest now?' the girls asked him.

'Not until the holds of my ship are filled with fine white salt,' he replied.

So they set to and ground out salt all night until dawn and then all day until sunset and the ship grew heavier and heavier until it was so full of salt it just sank.

Fenia and Menia are still grinding salt at the bottom of the ocean and that is why the sea is salty.

The water between Orkney and the mainland of Scotland is known as the Pentland Firth where there is the whirlpool called the Swelkie. That whirlpool is caused by the giant mill Grotti, turning, turning, turning.

The History of Kitty Ill Pretts

FIFE

Once there was a poor woman who had three daughters. No one remembers the names of the two eldest daughters but everyone remembers the name of the youngest, for she was called Kitty – Kitty Ill Pretts, since she loved to play pranks and was very, very clever.

The poor woman fell ill and since she knew she was dying she called her daughters to her bedside.

'When I am dead and gone I want you to go to the king's palace to find work for yourselves. Who knows but you may find your fortunes,' she said. 'To you my eldest daughter I leave my pot and to you my second daughter I leave my pan. But Kitty, all I can leave you is half a bannock and my blessing.'

So after the poor woman was dead and buried the three girls set off to the king's palace, but the two eldest sisters were jealous of clever Kitty and they did not want her to come with them. They even threw stones at her to send her home but Kitty would not turn back. Instead she took a different path through the forest and when the elder sisters arrived at the palace Kitty was already there waiting for them.

When the king heard there were three young girls looking for work he sent for them and asked the eldest sister, 'What can you do?'

She said, 'I can shape and I can shew, many a braw thing I can do.'

'Well, if you can cut and sew I shall send you to the seamstresses and you can make clothes,' said the king.

Then he asked the second sister, 'What can you do?'

She replied, 'I can bake and I can brew, many a braw thing I can do.'

'I like bread and beer so I shall send you to work in the kitchens,' said the king.

Last of all he asked Kitty, 'What can you do?'

And she answered, 'Oh, I can do all of those things and many more besides. I can turn the moon into cream cheese and take the stars from out of the skies.'

'Well I will have to think about a task for you Kitty,' said the king, 'but you can help your sisters in the meantime.'

So the king set them to work in the palace and very soon he realised that Kitty was indeed very clever. One day the king called for her.

'Kitty,' he said, 'there is a giant who lives across the Brig o' ae Hair, the Bridge of One Hair, and he has a most wonderful sword, a magic Sword of Light. Oh Kitty, how dearly I would love to have that sword and if you were to fetch it for me, why, I would marry my eldest son to your eldest sister.'

Now Kitty loved her sisters and she had long ago forgiven them and she wanted to make the king happy. She thought it would be a fine thing for her eldest sister to marry the prince and so she agreed. But before she left the palace, into the pockets of her apron she put some salt.

She set off and crossed the Brig o' ae Hair and she arrived at the giant's house. It was dark and through the window she could see the giant stirring a great pot of porridge over the fire. Every so often he tasted the porridge to see if it was just the way he liked it.

When Kitty saw this she climbed up on the roof and threw a handful of salt down the chimney into the giant's porridge.

The giant tasted his porridge again and said, 'It's too salty, it's too salty!'

Kitty threw more salt down the chimney and the giant stirred the porridge and tasted it once more, 'Arrrgh! This porridge is far too salty!' He called to the servant, 'Take the Sword of Light and go to the well to fetch me some water.'

The servant did as he was told and Kitty climbed down from the roof and crept behind him. When the servant stooped over the well to get the water, Kitty gave him a great push. He fell into the well but Kitty had grabbed the Sword of Light and she ran off as fast as she could.

The giant wondered why the servant was taking so long and he went to the door just in time to see Kitty running away. Off went the giant after Kitty, and he ran and she ran and soon Kitty was across the Brig o' ae Hair, BUT … as we all know a giant cannot cross a bridge of one hair. And this giant could not swim!

So Kitty got back to the palace and the king was happy and he married his eldest son to her eldest sister.

After a while, however, the king went to Kitty and said, 'Kitty, I wish you would help me again. That giant has a most beautiful horse with a saddle all hung with silver bells and I really would love to have that horse. If you will get it for me I will marry my second son to your second sister.'

Kitty thought it would be nice for her second sister to be married to the prince so she agreed to fetch the horse. But before she left, into the pockets of her apron she stuffed some straw.

She crossed the Brig o' ae Hair and arrived at the giant's stable. There she found the magnificent horse with its beautiful saddle and round and round she went stuffing each and every silver bell with straw to keep them from tinkling. When she was done she mounted the horse and rode as fast as she could but the straw fell out of one of the bells and it began to tinkle. The giant heard it and came out of the house and ran as fast as he could but not fast enough to catch Kitty. She was across the Brig o' ae Hair before him and of course, as we all know, a giant cannot cross a bridge of one hair.

So Kitty got back to the palace and the king was very happy indeed and he married his second son to her second sister.

For a long time the king seemed content but one day he went to Kitty and said, 'Kitty I won't be happy until I have one last thing from the giant. He has a beautiful bedspread, stitched with silver and gold and covered with precious stones and if you are clever enough to get this for me I shall marry you myself.'

Now Kitty thought it might be nice to marry the king for then she would be ... a queen! So she agreed. But, before she left, she slipped something into the pocket of her apron – I won't tell you what it was because I know you will guess for yourself later on.

She waited until it was dark and then crossed the Brig o' ae Hair and arrived at the giant's house. This time she went right into the house and hid under the bed with its beautiful cover. By and by the giant and his wife went to bed and fell asleep. Kitty reached out and gave the bedcover a pull.

'Be still,' said the angry giant and he gave his wife a great shove.

'It's not me, it's not me,' replied his wife meekly.

Kitty waited until they had gone back to sleep and she gave the bedcover another pull and again the giant roared at his wife to be still.

'It's not me, it's not me,' replied his wife, almost crying.

Again Kitty waited until they were asleep but this time she gave the bedcover such a great pull that it came off altogether and the giant woke up with a roar and jumped out of bed to see what was causing all the trouble.

Of course he soon found Kitty under the bed and he dragged her out by the hair on her head

and he was so stupid he actually asked Kitty
what he should do with her.

'Now Kitty if you were me and I was you,
what would you do with me?'

'Oh if I was you I would make me a big bowl
of porridge and make me eat it until it came
out of my eyes and my nose and my ears. Then
I would tie me up in a sack and I would go into
the forest and cut down a tree and bring it back
and then I'd beat the sack with it until I was
dead,' Kitty said.

'Well,' said the giant, 'that is what I shall do
to you.'

So he made a great bowl of porridge and
gave Kitty a spoon and he waited to see how
long it would be before it came out of her eyes
and her nose and her ears.

But clever Kitty said, 'I like honey on my
porridge,' and as soon as the giant turned away,
Kitty threw some of the porridge over her face
and when the foolish giant looked back he
really did think she'd eaten so much porridge
it was coming from out of her eyes and her
nose and her ears.

'Aha, Kitty Ill Pretts,' he laughed, 'I know what to do now!' and he put Kitty into a sack tied it up and went into the forest to chop down a tree.

As soon as he was gone, from out of her pocket Kitty took … a pair of scissors! She cut a hole in the sack and crept out. She caught the giant's wife, his cow, his pig, his ducks and hens, his dog and his cat and put them all into the sack and tied it up again. She bundled up the beautiful bedspread and ran off with it.

The giant returned to his house with a tree and he began to beat the sack. There was such a dreadful noise: the wife screamed, the cow moo'd, the pig squealed, the ducks quacked, the hens clucked, the dog barked and the cat mewed and they all cried out, 'It's me, it's me!'

'What a great noise you make Kitty! I know it's you,' said the silly giant and he just carried on beating that sack until at last his wife roared out.

'It's your wife in here you stupid great oaf! Kitty Ill Pretts tricked you!'

Now the giant was in such a rage he put on his seven league boots and ran after Kitty but

he arrived too late for Kitty was already on the
other side of the Brig o'ae Hair, quite safe, and
as we all know a giant cannot cross a bridge of
one hair.

'Oh Kitty,' said the stupid giant, 'tell me how
I can get over the river for I cannot cross the
bridge and I cannot swim.'

'Get a rope and tie a stone to one end of it
and tie a bag of gold in the middle of it and you
hold the other end. Then throw the end with
the stone to me and I shall pull you across the
river,' answered Kitty.

So the giant ran home and was back in no
time with the sack of gold and the rope. He did
just what Kitty had told him and tied a stone
on one end of the rope, the sack of gold in the
middle of the rope and he grabbed the other
end of it.

'Throw me the end with the stone,' called
Kitty, 'get into the river and I will pull you
across!'

The giant did as he was told and Kitty pulled
and pulled on the rope. She pulled and pulled
until she reached the sack of gold. She untied it

then she let the rope go and the giant fell over into the water and that was the end of him!

Kitty ran back to the palace with the gold and the beautiful bedspread all covered with jewels. The king was mighty pleased to have the magnificent bedspread and the sack of gold but he was even happier to have his clever Kitty home safe and sound.

So Kitty married the king and they lived happy and never drank from a dry cappy.

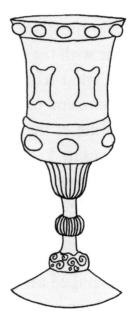

The King's Gift

LOWLANDS

One day King Malcolm was resting in his great hall at the end of a day's hunting when there was a knock at the door and his steward came in.

'Excuse me Sire, there is a man outside bringing you a gift,' he said.

King Malcolm liked nothing better than a gift and told the steward to show the man in. He was surprised to see such a poor looking man and even more surprised to be given such a lovely gift, a box carved with hunting scenes. There were huntsmen on horses with dogs running ahead chasing a stag, all beautifully carved round the edges of the box. As the king turned the box he heard something rattling inside. He lifted the lid and there was a silver bowl, beautifully decorated and inside the bowl he saw the words: '*Give this to the one you love.*'

It was a most unusual gift and he thanked the man and asked the steward to ensure he was given wine and a good meal.

During the evening the king looked at the gift again and again, admiring the fine carving on the box and thinking about those words inside the silver bowl. How he would love to keep it! But finally he knew what he had to do.

He loved the queen and so, in the morning, he asked his steward to take the gift to Queen Margaret, who was delighted to receive a gift from her husband. She looked at the box carved so beautifully with hunting scenes. She smiled for she knew how much the king loved hunting. Then she heard something rattle inside the box and when she opened it there she found the silver bowl. It was charming and when she looked inside she saw the words: '*Give this to the one you love.*'

The queen was puzzled for this was a gift she could not keep! All morning she wondered about those words until she knew what she had to do. She would give it to the Captain of the Guard for he served her faithfully and protected them all. She called for the steward who took the box to the Captain of the Guard.

The Captain of the Guard was very surprised to receive such a fine gift from the queen. He admired the finely carved box and when he opened it he found the silver bowl. Then he saw the words: '*Give this to the one you love.*'

He would really have liked to keep the queen's gift and all afternoon he wondered what to do until at last he knew. There was a pretty maid who worked in the kitchens and she always smiled so sweetly at him. So he took the box down to the kitchens and gave it to the maid who blushed with joy and bobbed him a curtsy, but the cook came by and sent him away.

The maid looked at the wonderful box. She had never received a gift before and this gift was special indeed. She looked at the carvings and opened the box and found the silver bowl. It was perfect but when she looked inside she saw scratching.

The cook looked over her shoulder and said, 'That is writing! There are words inside the bowl. Take it to the monk at the Abbey and he will read it to you.'

So the maid took it to the monk, who admired the extraordinary box and silver bowl and then he read the words: '*Give this to the one you love*.'

The maid returned to the castle and wondered what to do. She would like to keep this gift but she could not. She thought and thought until at last she knew just what to do.

The king was in the great hall seated by the fire when there was a knock at the door and his steward came in.

'Excuse me Sire, there is a maid outside bringing you a gift,' he said.

King Malcolm was surprised but he asked the steward to show the maid in and after she bobbed him a curtsey he asked her, 'Why would you bring me a gift?'

The maid replied, 'You have given me work, food and shelter and I am very happy here at the castle and I love my king.'

She gave the king the carved box and slipped out of the hall while he turned that box round and round admiring the fabulous hunting scenes. The king smiled as he opened the box and took out the silver bowl, glancing at the words inscribed inside. He walked over to the table and poured himself a glass of wine and he filled the silver bowl with water.

Then he gave it to his favourite hunting hound.

The Green Man of Knowledge

ABERDEENSHIRE

Jack lived with his mother, a widow who kept pigs, and while she worked hard, he did not. In fact Jack spent his days sitting beside the fire playing cards with his dog, a big old Highland Collie. No one could tell if the dog really played cards and of course people thought Jack was a nitwit, a fool with no sense at all.

On the day that Jack turned twenty-one he got up from the fireside and stretched. He was a tall young man and the clothes he had worn for years no longer fitted him, so he looked quite odd with his trousers up round his knees and his shirt sleeves at his elbows.

'Mother,' Jack said, 'away you go to feed your pigs. I'm away to seek my fortune.'

'Oh Jack, you daft laddie! You've never been past the gate and you'll get lost. Away and play with your doggie.'

Well they argued for a bit but when his mother had turned her back Jack was out of the house, across the farmyard and out of the gate. He was in an unknown world and he didn't know where he was or where to go, so he kept walking down the road until he reached a crossroads with a signpost. One of the signs read: *To the Land of Enchantment.* And that's the road Jack took.

Jack had been walking for some time and he was feeling very hungry, wishing now he had asked his mother for a bannock or something to eat along the way. Just ahead he saw a horse trough all covered with moss and when he reached it

he was pleased to see it was filled with water. There was a wee robin sitting on the edge. Jack bent down to take a drink.

'Hello Jack,' said the robin.

'Goodness me, a bird speaking! I've never heard a bird speak before. Why are you speaking?' asked Jack.

'Jack, you are in the Land of Enchantment where everyone can speak and understand each other – birds, animals and people,' said the robin.

'Well if I hadn't heard it with my own ears I never would have believed a bird could speak,' said Jack. 'But how do you know my name?'

'Oh Jack, we knew you were coming. We've been waiting twenty-one years for you,' said the robin.

'Well that was a long wait,' said Jack. 'You know what I'd like birdie,' he said, 'I could do with something to eat.'

'Follow me, Jack,' said the wee robin as it flitted off down the road.

They came to a lovely black-thatched cottage where an old woman sat rocking to and fro in a rocking chair. Jack thought she must be at least a hundred years old.

'Go on in and get your supper, Jack,' said the old woman.

So he went inside and what a sight met his eyes! There was a table laden with a bowl of hot, steaming porridge, the best he'd ever tasted, plates of scones and oatcakes and a great jug of ale, all served by the old woman's lovely granddaughter. When he could eat no more she asked if he would like to go to sleep, and of course he was very tired after his long walk, so she took him to a room with a great feather bed.

As soon as he lay down he was fast asleep, but he woke during the night and found he was lying on three peats covered with a sheepskin. Jack thought it was strange but it was still better than lying in the ashes beside the fire at his mother's house. However, in the morning he woke up in the fine feather bed.

'What a queer country this is,' thought Jack as he got up and went down to find breakfast ready for him.

'Before you leave, Jack,' said the young girl, 'go outside and my grandmother will give you some advice. In this land you will need all the advice you can get.'

So Jack greeted the old woman, 'Well, Grannie, how are you doing this morning?'

'I'm fine, Jack,' she replied. 'I must warn you as you go along the road today never talk to anybody first. Wait until they speak to you and then you can reply.'

So Jack thanked her and said goodbye and when he was just setting off the young girl gave him a parcel of scones.

Down the road went Jack and he walked and walked and walked and along the way he ate the scones. After a long while he heard bells, church bells, ringing away so sweetly and as he came up over the ridge he saw a pretty village. He opened up the parcel to finish the last of the scones and there he found a gold coin. He was surprised of course and he looked at it carefully and put it in his pocket before heading into the village.

Jack found an inn and, since he was feeling hungry again, ordered a big plateful of food and some home-brewed ale. While he was eating he noticed three men playing cards in the corner. They did not speak at all, just played cards. One of the men was dressed from head to toe in green and Jack could see from his face that he was a clever and cunning man. He wasn't a young man but he wasn't a very old man either, just a clever man with brains.

Jack forgot the old woman's advice not to speak first and went over to ask if he could get a game of cards with them.

'Have you got any money?' asked the man dressed in green and Jack showed him the change left over from his gold coin.

'Can you play cards?' he asked Jack, 'We don't play with men who cannot play cards.'

'Oh, I've practised a bit in my day,' said Jack, sitting down, and the four of them began to play. The clever man in green was a good card player but he couldn't beat Jack because Jack had practised all his life with his collie dog! Jack was winning all the money so the other two men left and Jack and the clever man played and played through the night until it was almost dawn.

Finally the man in green put down his cards, 'You are too good a man at cards for me,' he said. He got up and said, 'Goodbye Jack.'

'Wait a minute,' said Jack, 'you know my name. Who are you?'

'I'm the Green Man of Knowledge.'

'Where do you live?' asked Jack.

'East of the moon and west of the stars,' the man replied.

'That's a queer direction,' said Jack, but the man just left saying he could make what he wanted of it.

Jack had won heaps of money so he put some in his pocket and the rest into bags and asked the innkeeper to look after it while he went to find where the Green Man of Knowledge lived.

'Don't follow him,' said the innkeeper, shaking his head, 'you'll go to disaster if you follow him.'

But Jack was not worried and set off to follow, heading on down the road out of the village, and he walked and walked and walked until he came to a thatched cottage.

'Well this cottage is like the other one, so maybe they will help me on my way and I can pay them,' said Jack to himself as he knocked on the door.

'Come in, Jack!'

'Goodness,' said Jack, 'they are well informed in this country. Everyone knows my name.'

'I suppose you are hungry Jack so sit down and have something to eat,' said an old woman who was sitting in a rocking chair. She was even older than the first woman he'd met, maybe two hundred years old, knitting away making something round.

The meal was served by another young girl, ten times more bonnie than the first girl, and when Jack went to bed the same thing happened. The feather bed turned into peat when he lay down.

In the morning Jack saw that the old woman had finished her knitting and it lay on the floor and she said, 'I know you are looking for the Green Man of Knowledge so we are here to help you.'

'I'll take all the help I can get,' he said and after his breakfast the old woman gave him the piece of round knitting.

'Take it outside and lay it on the ground and sit on it. Sit cross-legged; cross your arms and whatever happens don't look behind you, Jack. If you look behind you it is the end. Say "*Away with you*" and it will take you where you need to go and when you land pick it up, whirl it three times round your head and say "*Home with you*" and it will come back to me.'

So Jack thanked the old woman, thinking this was very queer indeed. He did just as he was told, and soon he was flying so fast he could hardly breathe. He was dying to look back but he remembered what the old woman had told him and this time he did not ignore the advice and he kept looking forward. In no time at all he had landed and he was very pleased indeed to be standing on firm ground again. He took up the knitting and twirled it three times round his head, saying, 'Home with you', and off it went!

As Jack walked on he heard a ting-ting-ting and knew it was a blacksmith at work and soon he came to a house. Jack scratched his head, for there sitting rocking away was another old woman in a chair, even older than the last. If age counted in that land she was older!

'Well, well, Jack,' she said, 'we've been waiting for you. Go inside and get something to eat and have a good night's rest.'

Just as before, he had his meal and slept on a bed that changed from feathers to peat and in the morning the old woman told him to go to the smiddy shop where her husband had made something for him.

'Do as he tells you Jack and you won't go wrong,' she said.

The blacksmith had much to tell Jack. 'You are getting closer to the Green Man of Knowledge so you must remember he is a clever man and it won't be easy. There is a river to cross but I can't help you cross it. There is a bridge but if you step on that bridge it will turn to spiders' webs and you will fall through into the water. The water will turn to boiling lava and you would be instantly dead. There is only one person who can help you Jack.'

"And who would that be?' asked Jack.

'The Green Man of Knowledge has three daughters,' replied the smith, 'and the youngest one is the most powerful. It is she who will help you but you have to catch her first. They come down to the river each morning to swim and when they touch the water they turn into swans: two black swans and a white one. It is the white swan you must get, Jack. Hide near to the bridge and wait until they cross. See where they put their clothes and once they have become swans swimming you must pick up her clothes and everything that belongs to her. If you leave even a hairpin she will make a gown out of it and not help you at all.'

'Well, well,' said Jack, 'it's all very strange but I'll try it.'

The blacksmith gave Jack a very, very large horseshoe, 'Sit on the horseshoe, Jack, just as you did with the knitting, use the same words but whatever you do remember never look back.'

So Jack took the horseshoe and did as he was told, he never looked back and landed on the bank of a river. He twirled the mighty horseshoe over his head and sent it back home like before and then he hid and waited by the bridge. Soon afterwards three beautiful girls came tripping over the bridge towards him and Jack saw that the youngest one was the most lovely. He was careful to notice what she was wearing and then, when he saw two black swans and a white swan swimming, he went to find their clothes. He gathered up all the clothes of the youngest, even her ribbons and hairclips and hid them.

After a while the two black swans went to the bank to get dressed and they crossed back across the bridge as young ladies but the white swan called out, 'Where are you Jack? I need my clothes. Surely you are a gentleman.'

Jack called back, 'I was well warned about you and I'm no gentleman. I'm just Jack the Fool. If you want your clothes you'll have to carry me across the river. It's a cruel thing to ask but I know you can do this.'

'Sit on my back then Jack,' she said, 'but for your sake and mine you must not tell my father how you crossed this river.'

So Jack promised and she opened up her wings and Jack sat on her back and she took him across the river and when he landed he left her clothes on the dry bank.

Jack walked up to the castle but before he got there the girl ran past him away round to the back as he knocked on the door. The Green Man of Knowledge was flabbergasted … shocked!

'How did you get here? How did you cross the river?'

'Oh I came the way you come but I flew across the river,' said Jack as cool as can be.

'You have no wings, Jack.'

'Ah,' said Jack, 'I can grow wings if I want to; nothing is impossible.'

'Well, Jack, come in,' he said, 'I must shake your hand.' But as he reached for Jack's hand he gave him a push and Jack fell down through a trap door into a wee room, fine for a mouse but not big enough for a man like Jack. 'Eat, drink and be merry,' laughed the Green Man of Knowledge.

'A lad would not be merry on this!' said Jack as he looked at the cup of water and the green, mouldy bit of bread in the room. Then the trapdoor shut.

After a while Jack heard a whisper, 'Jack, I've come to help you. My father is evil and when you caught me you broke the spell and now I am free to love you and to help you.' It was the youngest daughter. She gave him some food, a fine feast it was, and warned him to be careful since her father was a cruel man.

In the morning the Green Man of Knowledge opened up the door and asked how Jack was after the night. Jack said he had been well fed and had never slept so well.

'Well you are easy to please, Jack,' he said, letting Jack out of the hole, 'I shall set you three tasks. Firstly, tomorrow you must go down the deep well to find my wife's ring. It's easy enough and I could do it but I want to see what kind of man you are.'

Jack peered down the deep dark well and saw it was dry and he wondered how he could get down and back up. Jack was still wondering what to do that night while shut up in the wee room when he heard White Swan whispering to him. That's what he called her, White Swan.

She brought him food again and told him that the task should be impossible but that she would help him. 'I will turn myself into a ladder, Jack, from the top to the bottom. I will make the muddy bottom clear as crystal so you can find the ring, but Jack please be very careful as you climb for if you miss a step you will break a bone in my body.

In the morning the Green Man of Knowledge took Jack to the well. Jack peered over the edge and felt for the ladder and then he hopped over and cried out pretending he was falling. But all the time he was stepping down the ladder and sure enough at the bottom he could see the ring. He missed his step once and thought sadly he might have broken the girl's neck. He reached for the ring, put it into his pocket and very, very carefully climbed back up wondering how badly hurt she must be.

'You are a clever man, Jack,' said the Green Man of Knowledge, 'so give me the ring.'

But Jack would not. 'I did the work so I will keep the ring.'

'Someone is helping you, Jack! Who is it?'

Jack said nothing of course and so the Green Man of Knowledge shut him up in the little room again and Jack wondered about the second task. White Swan came to him with food that night and Jack was very pleased to see her.

'I thought I had broken your neck,' he said.

'One more step and that would have been true but you did break my little pinkie. So I wore gloves at dinner and my father did not see. We are safe for now. But tomorrow, Jack, he wants you to build a castle out of nothing in only one hour.'

'Goodness,' said Jack, 'I couldn't thatch a roof in three months, let alone build a castle in an hour.' But he knew White Swan would be there to help him.

In the morning the Green Man of Knowledge asked how he spent the night and Jack said he had spent a fine night and that he liked this castle.

'If you like this castle then here is your next task. I want you to build a castle finer than this on the other side of the hill and I will give you one hour,' said the Green Man of Knowledge.

'Right,' said Jack, 'away with you then because I cannot work if anyone is watching.'

Jack looked around for White Swan but she did not appear. He sat down and worried and fretted thinking how he would be a dead man soon and then, just when he thought he should make his escape, he heard her. He turned around and there she was and behind her was the most magnificent castle.

But then he saw a hole in its wall.

'Oh lassie, that hole is as big as a house, it's a mistake,' said Jack, 'he will see me dead for this.'

'It is no mistake, Jack. When he asks about it tell him you left it for him to fill up and see what he says. You are safe so long as you do not tell him who is helping you.'

The Green Man of Knowledge was mighty surprised to find the castle and he walked round it until he found the hole.

'So you could not complete the task!' he said.

'I left that so you could fill it,' Jack replied.

The Green Man of Knowledge again asked who was helping him but Jack told him he only had an old collie dog for a friend.

'Well, Jack, your last task will be to clear all the ants from the wood in thirty minutes and if you can do this you can have as much money as you can carry and any of my daughters as a wife. And you will have your freedom again.'

'I'd like my freedom since I have an old mother working with pigs. I'd like to go back home and help her and see my old doggie too. So off you go while I get on with the job,' said Jack.

How she did it Jack never knew but White Swan had the job done in thirty minutes and was gone just as the Green Man of Knowledge returned.

'You are a clever man, Jack,' he said and this time he took Jack back to his castle and gave him a fine meal in the great hall. Then he gave him four bags of gold and asked Jack to come out to the stables where he kept a herd of fine horses, all of them mares.

As Jack was walking he heard White Swan whispering, 'Jack, take the old donkey – take the old donkey.'

When Jack arrived at the stables he saw the most beautiful horses, each one strong enough to carry him and the gold. He looked at the poor wee donkey and thought it could not carry the gold let alone carry him as well. The donkey looked at him and he knew what he had to do.

'I'll take the wee donkey,' he said, 'she'll be fast enough for poor Jack.'

The Green Man of Knowledge was angry and said he should take one of the horses rather than be shamed riding through the countryside on such a poor old nag. But Jack loaded the gold on to the back of the donkey and when the donkey hee-hawed he sat upon her and away they went.

Jack knew this was really White Swan helping him again and he called to her to slow down for fear she might kill herself running so fast. But no sooner had he said this than they realised the Green Man of Knowledge was riding hard behind them.

'Jack, I can't run fast enough. Take a drop of water from my left ear and throw it behind you. Ask for rivers and lakes behind us and a clear road ahead of us.'

Jack did this and saw the rivers and lakes and asked the wee donkey to rest up a bit but she said no, for the Green Man of Knowledge was riding a fine black mare, one of her wicked sisters. So she ran and ran until she called to Jack, 'Take a stone from my right ear and throw it behind us and ask for mountains, hills and dales behind us and a clear road ahead of us.'

Jack did as she told him but over the mountains and hills and through the dales the

Green Man of Knowledge was soon upon them and all the while the wee donkey ran and ran until Jack feared for her life.

'Jack, I love you,' she cried out, 'and I will destroy the Green Man of Knowledge but it will put a spell on us both. Look in my left ear and take the spark of fire. Throw it behind you and ask for a wall of fire behind us and a clear road ahead.'

Jack did as she said and when he looked around the Green Man of Knowledge rode into the wall of fire and disappeared. As soon as that happened the wee donkey turned into the young girl again and Jack was standing on his own two feet holding the four bags of gold.

'Now, Jack, because of this I must leave you for a year, but one year from today I will come for you. In all that time you must not let anyone kiss you, not even your mother,' the girl told him, 'for if anyone kisses you then you will be under a spell and you will forget me. Don't let anybody kiss you Jack.'

'I won't let anyone kiss me,' said Jack, 'and I will be waiting for you.'

Jack set off down the road thinking a year is not too long and of course he had all that gold. Soon he realised he was very close to home and in no time at all he hopped over the fence and his mother rushed out so happy to see him. She was trying to kiss him of course but Jack was having none of that. So he went into the house and there was his big old collie dog wagging his tail and he jumped up, put his paws on

Jack's chest and gave him a big lick. That was it! In that instant Jack forgot everything.

Jack had plenty of money so people said Sir Jack this, and Sir Jack that, instead of calling him Jack the Fool, since money seems to make a difference. He bought a big house and was working away at a new business and doing very well even though he could not read or write. After some months Jack and the miller's daughter walked out together and soon enough they were engaged to be married.

The day of the wedding was exactly one year after Jack came home and while the guests gathered he was still busy in his office when a young girl knocked on the back door. Though she was dressed in a torn skirt and a tattered blouse she was very beautiful and she asked for a job.

'What can you do?' asked the cook.

She said she could cook and clean and so the cook took her on to help with the wedding and to stay on after the wedding to clear up after the guests. She was set to washing dishes while they waited for the preacher but time passed and the preacher was late.

The guests were getting impatient and Jack's mother wondered what could be done to keep everyone happy. She went to those working in the kitchen and the ragged girl spoke up.

'I can do a trick with my wooden cockerel and my wooden hen, they can peck and talk and that might amuse everyone until the preacher arrives.'

So Jack's mother took her to the guests, all dressed in their fine clothes, and the ragged girl set the wooden cockerel and hen on the floor and scattered some corn. Jack came out to watch while they pecked and picked up the corn. Then everyone was amazed when the hen spoke to the cockerel. 'Do you remember me, Jack?' she said.

The cockerel looked at the hen and replied, 'Remember you? No I can't say that I do,' and he went on picking up the corn.

The hen asked, 'Do you remember the Green Man of Knowledge?'

'The Green Man of Knowledge? No I don't remember him,' said the cockerel.

'Do you remember me, Jack, the woman you love?' she asked.

'Ah … no, sorry, I don't remember you.'

'Well, Jack, do you remember the little donkey that saved your life and destroyed the Green Man of Knowledge?' said the wooden hen.

The cockerel stopped pecking at the corn and looked at the hen, 'Yes I do remember.'

Jack looked at the wooden hen and then he looked at the ragged girl and thought of the wee donkey, 'I do remember! I remember you!' he shouted out.

He hugged and kissed the lassie and told the surprised guests the whole story I have told you, and that took a long time didn't it!

By the end of the story the preacher had arrived, the miller's daughter became a bridesmaid and Jack married the girl he still called White Swan.

Glossary

a'	all
ae	one
bannock	a round flat cake, often made with oats and baked over the fire
birled	whirled around
braw	fine
brig	bridge
byres	cow sheds, barns
burn	a stream
cappy	cup, used to rhyme with happy. If your cup is never dry you are well off
clotis	clots
corbie	raven
dirk	a short dagger, part of Highland dress
drap	drop
each uisge	Gaelic, meaning water horse
faem	foam
fra	from

gae	go
garris	from gar, meaning to make
glen	a narrow valley
gloaming	twilight
gowd	gold
guidman	a polite way to address a man – the head of a household
guidwife	a polite way to address a woman – mistress of a house
haif	have
hame	home
hinnie	honey
ill	'ill woman'; troublesome; ill pretts – mischievous pranks
ken	know
kirk	church
kist	a large storage box
lang	long
laird	lord of an estate
lassie	an unmarried girl
mester	master
nightis	nights
orra	unskilled or casual worker
peat	rotting material dug from moorland to be dried for use as fuel for fires

piece	food, usually a snack or sandwich
plaid	a length of woollen cloth worn as clothing
pretts	pranks or tricks
quern	a hand mill made of stone
quhare	where
quhat	what
sault	salt
scantlie	from scant, meaning a small amount; Scantlie Mab – Little Mab
shape	cut a pattern or material for clothes
shew	sew
smiddy	blacksmith or blacksmith's workshop
spaeman	wise man
stoor worm	a wild or ferocious dragon
sweit	sweat
thrapple	windpipe
trews	trousers
womyne	woman
wynd	a narrow street
yer	your

Notes

The Witch of Fife
In 1819 James Hogg published *The Queen's Wake: A Legendary Poem*, a collection of ballads that includes The Witch of Fife. James Hogg, known as the Etterick Shepherd, wrote in both English and Scots.

Old Croovie
For all of the wonderful stories told by Stanley Robertson he is remembered most for this story. Jack is the hero of the Travellers and if you retell this story it is important not to change it, and don't forget the ball of wool was blue!

The Midwife's Tale
Stories like this can be found across Europe. In Scotland there is a similar story called *Nurse Kind and Ne'er Want* from Nithsdale but for

years I have shaped and told my version set in the Old Town of Edinburgh.

Thomas the Rhymer

Thomas lived approximately between 1210 and 1290 and Ercildoune is today known as Earlston, near Melrose. One of his predictions foretold the Battle of Bannockburn in 1314 when Robert the Bruce defeated the English:

The Burn of Breid	The Burn of Bread … (Bannockburn)
Shall rin fou reid	Shall run full red … (with blood)

Why the Sea is Salty

Usually regarded as a Scottish story this is actually a story from Iceland and found in Snorri Sturluson's book *The Prose Edda*.

The Green Man of Knowledge

In 1954 Geordie Stewart recorded this story for Hamish Henderson who was collecting stories from the Travellers. Geordie Stewart was a young man at the time and he had learned it from his grandfather. It can be regarded as a Stewart family story.

The Scottish Storytelling Centre is delighted to be associated with the *Folk Tales* series developed by The History Press. Its talented storytellers continue the Scottish tradition, revealing the regional riches of Scotland in these volumes. These include the different environments, languages and cultures encompassed in our big wee country. The Scottish Storytelling Centre provides a base and communications point for the national storytelling network, along with national networks for Traditional Music and Song and Traditions of Dance, all under the umbrella of TRACS (Traditional Arts and Culture Scotland). See www.scottishstorytellingcentre.co.uk for further information. The Traditional Arts community of Scotland is also delighted to be working with all the nations and regions of Great Britain and Ireland through the *Folk Tales* series.

Donald Smith
Director, Tracs
Traditional Arts and Culture Scotland